The Porch

A novel by
Rachel Hope Turany Mendell

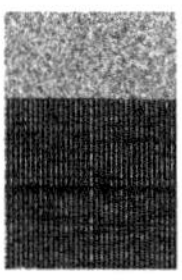

Snow Dragon 2022

To Mosaic Mansfield

A white-haired old man sits in a dark, ancient, hand-carved rocker on his expansive white front porch enjoying the early morning.

He sips coffee out of a hefty white mug with the words "The Boss" printed in big black letters. He is waiting for what he knows will come. Next to him on the table is a cold cherry wood pipe in a carved, chipped terra cotta ash holder. Next to that a worn chess set is ready for play.

He looks to the right, passed an eclectic collection of well-used patio furniture filling the 40-foot planked floor, into deep woods, cool and green. He looks to the left, over the white-washed railing, past climbing vines, over the narrow dirt road that leads away from the Big House into the fields and out to the rest of the world. In front of him the lush grassy meadow looks like it goes on forever.

Sometimes as the old man rocks, he gazes out into the future. Sometimes he sits and talks with the workers on his ranch. Sometimes he plays word games with the small children that come to sit on his lap, and he asks them about life. The aromas of coffee, fresh bread, cinnamon, and fried sausage escape through an open window behind him. Pots and pans clank and scrape while the faucet hushes "shsht" on and off. Snippets of conversation and laughter flutter from doorways and paths behind the huge white house.

The old man sits up in his chair. Yes! There he is.

That small dot rising above the horizon, growing slowly, bobbing up and down. This is what he has been waiting for. Someone is walking upward toward the house. A figure emerges.

Suddenly, the old man seems to become young as he springs to his feet and jumps off the steps like a college cross country athlete. The young man pauses when he sees the old man coming. He seems to struggle, unable to move faster. People gather to watch from the house.

The young man and the old man meet on the grassy hill. The young man falls to the ground. The words they exchange float on the breeze and away into the trees.

The old man pulls the young man into a hug. They hold on to each other for a long time. Then they turn and walk slowly toward the house, the weak leaning on the strong. The cheering inside the house grows. The cook in the kitchen is calling for help.

It's time to celebrate.

Chapter 1

Nate woke up in a room that looked like Aunt Betsie's spare room upstairs – the one he used to use for naps when he was a kid. The bed was comfortable, but his head was fuzzy, as if a headache was just around the corner, waiting to attack. He lay still just in case. He focused on the smooth ceiling, white, no cobwebs or dust, no random marks from spit wads or pencils or gum; just white and gleaming. It was comforting somehow to look at a clean ceiling. He couldn't remember seeing one before. Not even in a hotel.

He gently moved his head to the left. The walls were blue, just like Aunt Betsie's walls, except they were cleaner and brighter somehow, like whoever painted it had used a nicer shade of blue, or maybe no one had ever smoked in this room.

It looked like Aunt Betsie's, but it didn't feel like Aunt Betsie's.

He eased his head to the right. There was the door – an old door with a wood frame from the early 1900s. A feeling of old strength filled the room. The door wasn't off-center like Aunt Betsie's. This door was hung as straight as he had ever seen. He thought it would be a pleasure to give it a fresh coat of paint, even though it didn't need one.

His head had cleared. He sat up with ease. He felt

pretty good, in fact, better than he had in months.

He looked down at his clothes, jeans, blue t-shirt, hoodie, and tried to remember how he got there. He closed his eyes. No memories came – none at all. A tiny ball of fear sparked in his middle.

Beside the door was an old chest of drawers and next to that a small set of shelves. On the opposite wall was a big window with white fluttering drapes and lowered blinds. Above the bed was a high undraped window with late afternoon orange light streaming in.

He got off the bed, which squeaked just a little, but not in an annoying way. He opened the blinds and saw a large expanse of deep green lawn broken by a large beige three story building off to the right and woods beyond that. He saw people coming and going from the front door of the building and movement in a few of the windows. Everyone seemed happy and busy.

He wondered why he cared. He hadn't cared about much of anything for a long time. But he couldn't remember why.

What was he doing here? And where was here? He tried out the chair by the window. It was comfortable, like it was made for him. On the nightstand next to the chair was a blue book. It looked old and boring, like the books he hadn't read at school.

Nate looked around and felt like he was supposed to go somewhere. He got up from the chair and laid back down on the bed. When in doubt, take a nap. He closed his eyes.

After a few moments he sat straight up in a panic, a spark fluttering in his belly. Work! Wherever he was, he was late!

Why hadn't the alarm gone off? He dug in his pocket for his cell phone – gone. He checked for his wallet – also gone. On a hunch he checked the top drawer in the nightstand. Yup. There they were. He took a deep breath and tried to think.

His cheap phone was off. He turned it over. The

battery was gone. His wallet was empty. No money. No ID. He checked the other drawers – nothing, just some clothes.

There was a knock at the door. He waited. They didn't come in. He heard voices outside in the yard. He heard more voices in the hallway. Another knock.

Nate opened the door.

"Hey, Nate, you're looking better!"

"Who -"

"Oh, so you don't remember yet."

Nate suddenly felt the spark turn to a stab of fear, like he had done something wrong and couldn't remember what it was.

"I came to get you for dinner. Think you could eat?"

"Sure, uh, I forgot your name. Sorry."

"Joe."

Nate followed the lanky energetic young man out the door.

"I don't have the keys," he said searching his empty pockets.

"Don't need 'em."

"Shouldn't I lock it?"

"Na. No one is going in your room but you."

"Where are we?"

"We'll talk at dinner."

Once in the hall, Nate noticed everything was clean and pleasant. On the walls were paintings of all styles, some he recognized. A wide wooden staircase descended gently into a huge living room. People were seated here and there, talking, and reading. There was a small fire in the fireplace.

At the bottom they turned to the left and entered the biggest kitchen Nate had ever seen.

"Cook, this is Nate."

A tall woman turned from looking out of the window, wiped her large hands on her apron and said, "Hi, Nate. I'm Pearl. Ya'll can call me Cook. Everyone does.”

“Hi,” said Nate.

“Look how skinny you are! You gotta eat,” Cook commanded. “Sit down over there. I'll fix you something.”

“Cook is the best,” said Joe, leading Nate to a push-through counter with bar stools. “She knows what people like even before they ask.”

Cook's laugh sounded like deep molasses. “Don't believe 'em Nate. I just knows my job is all.”

Nate smiled despite trying not to. He was hungry.

Cook laid a plate before Joe with a piece of pecan pie and a fork. Nate's stomach grumbled.

“I already had dinner,” said Joe as he dug in.

Cook laid a plate in front of Nate. On it was sliced turkey, mashed potatoes, and corn. It smelled wonderful. Nate felt a lump of some strong emotion coming to the surface. Why should he want to cry over a plate of food?

“Prayers, boys,” said Cook.

“Oh, yeah,” said Joe. “Sorry, Nate, I always forget.”

He bowed his head and said, “God, we thank you for this food. It smells really really good!”

Nate whispered, “Amen.” He looked around trying to figure out where he was. This wasn't home. He would know if he was home, right? Where was he?

Five minutes later Cook took the empty plates and brought back seconds. Even in his uneasiness, Nate was still hungry. He ate like he hadn't eaten in days. Stuffed, he leaned back and sighed.

“What did I tell you?” said Joe. “She's the best cook ever!”

Cook laughed a big jolly laugh. Nate was nodding his head in agreement.

“Ready for the tour?” asked Joe.

“Sure,” said Nate feeling good. Really good. Happy. He had never felt this good in his entire life, almost too good to be true.

Joe led Nate out the front door and on to the porch. A few people were sitting in chairs and benches. To the left was a stocky, white-haired old man rocking in the biggest mahogany rocking chair he had ever seen. It fit him like it was made for him. The old man stopped rocking and smiled.

"Did you eat, Nate?" asked the old man.

Nate nodded. Joe whispered in his ear, "Sir."

"Oh," said Nate. "Yes, Sir."

"Good. Good."

Before Nate could ask the question in his mind, a slightly stooped man in olive work clothes approached the old man from the yard below. "All done, Sir," he said.

"That's fine, Henry. Fine. You get yourself some dinner now."

"Yes, Sir. Thank you, Sir."

"Then a game of chess?"

"Sure thing! I mean ... if you like getting beat!"

The men laughed. Nate moved to the steps to leave, but Joe held his arm.

"You're going to like it here, Nate," said the old man.

Nate wanted to say, "Where is here?" but he couldn't get the words out.

"Joe, you show him around and give him a job."

"Sure, Ken. Will do," said Joe. "C'mon, Nate."

Joe jumped off the stairs and walked away. Nate looked from Joe to the old man. The old man smiled, and his fluffy white beard expanded. Nate smiled back even though he tried not to.

"You called him Ken ..." said Nate catching up with Joe.

"Oh, yeah," said Joe. "Me and The Old Man go way back."

Nate studied Joe. He must be in his twenties, thought Nate, like me. How "way back" could that be?

"Where are we?" Nate finally got the words out.

"We call it The Ranch," said Joe.

The big white house was surrounded by large trees, not enough to block any windows from perfect views, but large enough to provide lots of shade. Nate thought the trees were the biggest he had ever seen.

Joe paused in the front lawn and pointed up the gentle slope that led to the large expanse of mowed meadow that seemed to go on and on forever.

"That's where we came from last night. Remember?"

Nate tried but couldn't. "No," he said, shaking his head. Nate thought it should bother him that he couldn't remember, but it didn't. He felt so good.

"Well, you will. When you do, you might want to come find me. I'm in the sixth room on the first floor just in case you need something. Okay?"

"Sure," said Nate.

Around the west side of the house Joe pointed at the large three-story building, the one Nate had seen from his window. "That's what we call the Rest House. There's a doctor there and some other people that can help you if you get hurt."

"Wow," said Nate. "Like your own hospital?"

"Something like that."

"You ever had to go there?"

"No, not yet. But I'm glad it's there just in case, you know?"

Nate nodded. They stopped in the back of the house.

"It looks so much bigger from the back," said Nate.

"The Big House has two floors with lots of bedrooms for a lot of the people who live and work here."

A little farther and Joe pointed out the stables. Men and women were working with the horses and Nate could just make out a track past the row of trees beyond.

"Maybe they'll let me ride a horse," said Nate, feeling even better.

"Maybe," said Joe. He opened the back door of the Big House. Inside and to the right was a large closet used for household cleaning supplies. Joe grabbed a broom and handed it to Nate.

"Do you know how to sweep?"

"Yeah," said Nate, "Doesn't everybody?"

"Ken told me to give you a job and I think this would be good for starters. Just sweep all the hallways on the first floor."

"All?"

"Well, there's not much to do," said Joe. "When you are finished you can do what you want."

"Okay," said Nate. Joe exited out the rear door.

Nate began sweeping half-heartedly, feeling a little humiliated. He had hoped the "tour" would take longer. There seemed to be so much more to this new place. He had seen some other buildings off through the trees. He didn't recognize anything.

All the floors were polished wood. It seemed as if they had recently been swept, but Nate swept them anyway. After about 15 minutes he had developed a pile of sweepings. He went back for a dustpan.

After 30 minutes Nate realized he was enjoying himself. The irritating feeling of not knowing where he was faded.

He found some corners further on that had been missed by the last person who swept, and he felt a crisp sense of pride, something he had not felt in a long time.

He came around again to the broom closet. He put the broom and pan away. Walking out the rear door, he didn't know what else to do. So, he made his way back to his room.

No one was on the front porch. No one met him on the stairs or in the hallway. As he entered his room, he smelled something he recognized from many years ago –

vanilla maybe, or cookies baking. The light in his room seemed more subdued as the sun set. His room seemed bigger somehow. But he must be tired and imagining things.

Then he spotted it: a plate of cookies, a glass of cold milk and the book on his nightstand. He curled up in the reading chair and ate every cookie ... there were seven ... as he explored the book. Soon he was bored and put the book back on the table. Suddenly tired, he crawled back into bed and fell asleep.

The next morning Nate rolled out of bed refreshed. But he was troubled. He had had one of those emotional dreams where he couldn't recall the details. He was running somewhere. He thought about finding Joe and asking him where the showers were, but then gave that up in search of food.

In the kitchen, Cook was at the stove. He noticed an open pass-through on the far side of the kitchen leading into a huge dining room. There were other people eating in there; people he didn't know. Nate felt that small ball of fear in his gut again. Was he late?

"Hungry?" asked Cook.

"Yes," said Nate.

"You can keep me company. Grab yourself something and come sit over here." It was as if Cook could read his mind. He wasn't late. He hadn't made a mistake. Nate felt a wave of relief.

Breakfast was eggs fixed in a variety of ways, crisp bacon, hot sausage, soft biscuits, hash browns and fresh fruit. He tried not to over-fill his plate, but he was so hungry. He sat and ate, trying to take his time.

"So, what you up to today?" asked Cook.

Nate swallowed. "I did some sweeping yesterday. But today I don't know."

"I'm sure you'll find something to do. There's always plenty of work."

Nate ate silently. When he was finished, he got up.

"Plate," said Cook.

"What?"

"Wash your things. We all do our part around here."

"Oh. Where?"

Cook nodded in the direction of the sink full of hot sudsy water. Nate could remember washing dishes, but where he didn't know. He washed and dried his things and stacked them with the rest on the sideboard. He walked over to where Cook was pealing more potatoes.

"How long have you been here?" he asked.

"Just about my whole life."

"You were born here?"

"Well, I don't rightly know about that. Can't remember where I was born. Doesn't matter. I love it here. It's my home."

"Do you always cook?"

"Yes, I love cooking. It's what I do. I do other things, you know, to stretch myself, but cooking is what I love."

"Aren't there other cooks? People who help you with all the work?"

"Oh, yes, they're here. You'll see them."

Nate thought about that for a minute. "Don't you get bored? Don't you ever want to leave?"

"I got bored twice. I went for a walk both times, leaving out the back door."

"The back door?"

"Yup. Ask around. They'll show it to you. But if you really want to leave, you won't have to ask, you'll find it yourself. Just remember: You might leave out the back door, but you always come back in the front."

"It seems like such a nice place. Why would anyone want to leave?"

"How long you been here, Child?"

"This is ... well, I think it's my second day. But I can't remember when I got here."

"Oh, I see. You can't remember your other life yet."

"My other life?" said Nate, that ball of fear starting to grow in his gut again. He felt his face getting hot, like when he got in trouble with ... someone.

"You'll remember it soon enough. Everyone does in their own time. When I remember I wished I could forget. I came from a bad, bad place. I don't think about it much anymore, and if I ever do, like if something some newbie says to me reminds me of it, I'm just so thankful that I'm here. Then I forget all about it again."

"You came from a very bad place? Where was that?"

"That is a discussion for another day, Mr. Nate. Right now, you need to shower. Whew!"

"Oh," Nate was suddenly embarrassed. "I don't ..."

Cook pointed her knife and looked at Nate straight on. "Okay. Here's what you do. Go back to your room and gather your things for a shower. Then go out to the hall and look for a door that says 'showers' or maybe it will say 'bathroom'. It's different for everyone."

This all sounded strange to Nate, like a different language. But he said, "Good morning" and did as he was told.

Back in his room there were towels and wash clothes waiting for him, along with all the shower things he liked, including soap-on-a-rope. He wasn't sure why he liked it. He just knew he did. It smelled exactly right.

He walked out the door and to the left toward the back of the house. Sure enough, posted on a door was a nice professional looking blue sign with white writing: "Showers." Something clicked inside his brain, a tiny memory, something uncomfortable, like he didn't like showers for some reason. But he wanted to please Cook. He liked her. He trusted her. She was the best cook ever.

The shower room was warm, smelled of soap and lemon, and felt private. Each of the ten stalls had locks on them and only the slightest bit of floor was seen under the doors, which were eight feet tall. He chose the seventh one. There were others in use, judging from the spraying sound all around. There were no signs warning him about excessive hot water use or time limits or horseplay or noise. Everything was tiled in rich blues and greens. Inside the stall there was a bench, a mirror, a sink, and a toilet – all contained in the room. It was an individual bathroom all to himself ... and the door locked. He suddenly felt much better. The shower head was perfect. The temperature, after a little adjustment was perfect. The shower stream was perfect. He was torn between pleasure and guilt, between taking the longest shower of his life and taking a very short one. He settled on washing until he was finished with a minute of letting the hot water run on his back.

Once dressed, he unlocked the door and timidly looked out. There were still people showering, but no one was in the main room. Grateful, he gathered his things and went back to his room.

He noted the laundry basket in the corner. He hadn't seen it there. He placed his clothes in it and wondered if he would have to find a laundromat.

He sat on his chair and listened to the breeze in the trees. He pulled his knees up to his chin and smiled. After talking to Cook he wondered when he would remember where he had been before this place. He wondered how horrible it must have been for him to forget it so completely. He didn't want to think about it. The thought of a hidden life frightened him. He closed his eyes, listened to the voices outside and fell asleep again.

Chapter 2

It was late afternoon when Nate woke up. The slanting rays of the sun illumined his window, and he had that old feeling of being late for something. He left his room and made his way slowly down the hall feeling a little lost. It seemed wider than before, and he noticed the carpet was turquoise. He identified the artwork on the walls. He stood in front of one and named it out loud: "'Starry Night' by Van Gogh." A tiny memory flickered in his mind, something from school.

He noticed how the big lumps of bright paint swirled with the stars and the moon and the wind blowing in the trees. He touched the bumps. They were real. But that couldn't be right. This painting couldn't be an original. The original was in New York. Then he wondered how he knew that.

He walked toward the back of the house studying the art on the walls and the sculpted pieces placed on shelves and podiums in recessed areas along the length of the hall. He passed a room that had quiet contemplative music. The next room played Top 40s. At the far end of the hall was a large window overlooking the back yard where people seemed to be setting up for a picnic. He could hear Asian meditation music and strong African drumming coming from other rooms. He closed his eyes and picked out Dixieland, Rock and Roll and Mardi Gras blues.

Nate turned right and walked up the parallel hallway on the other side of the house, pausing for a moment by each door. He heard old-fashioned Big Band music, heavy metal and a strange something that was pleasant, but unlike anything he had ever heard. The hallway seemed to go on and on. He heard quiet conversations, laughter and crying. Nate felt as if he was once again in a building he had never been in before.

Turning a corner once again, he passed the front staircase and walked back down the first hall. Nate came to his door, almost unwilling to leave the experience. He heard music from inside his room. He didn't remember seeing a radio or music player. He opened the door to his most favorite song ever. His throat tightened. He closed his door, flopped on his bed, and cried.

The song ended and Nate realized he was hungry again. From his window he heard the sizzling of meat, laughter, and conversation. Wiping his eyes, Nate left his room and walked down the front staircase. Several people were sitting and talking, several were playing cards, some reading.

Suddenly, Joe was at his side. "Hey, Nate. You like burgers?"

"Yeah," said Nate, happy to see him.

"Come on down. We're grilling outside. There's plenty of food." Joe took Nate by the arm and pulled him down the stairs. He was excited which made Nate excited.

Suddenly remembering, Nate said, "Joe ... your room?"

"Oh, yeah. Forgot to show you. Well, it's on the first floor. Sixth door on the right. You can't miss it. There's a big sign with my name on it."

Once outside they were lost in a crowd of joyful, laughing, talking, joking people.

Joe tugged Nate's arm. "The food is over here," he

said. Soon they were standing in line with large heavy dinner plates gazing at a long table filled with the most delicious looking food Nate had ever seen. Joe heaped his plate. Nate took small portions and was careful not to spill anything. Joe led him to one of the tables. Everyone at the table greeted Joe and Nate by name. Nate wondered how they knew who he was. He didn't know anyone but Joe, Cook and the old man. Oh, and Henry.

He ate quietly and slowly, listening to the conversation around him.

He didn't understand much of what they were talking about, but the people were happy, and they smiled at Nate as if they knew him and he belonged.

At the end of the table an older lady looked at Nate and smiled. Nate smiled back despite himself. There was something familiar about the lady, her blue gingham dress, her blue eyes. Suddenly, a huge well of ache grew in his gut and he felt like he was going to cry again. He looked down at his plate and forced it to pass.

Joe noticed. "You okay? You look like you don't feel too good."

"I'm fine," croaked Nate.

Everyone knew Joe and he talked to everyone, even people in the next table over. Nate started to feel invisible – a familiar, humiliating feeling. The more Joe laughed and talked to other people; the deeper Nate fell into his excludedness.

After a few moments Nate got up and left. The pleasant voices and wonderful aromas followed him. He felt small, like he had done something wrong, and people were making fun of him, and he didn't know why, and he didn't care. Nate felt confused by his embarrassment, then frustrated and soon he was angry. He stomped up the front steps.

The old man was waiting for him. "Had enough to eat?"

Nate made a non-committal sound and shrugged

his shoulders.

"Nate," said the old man. Something in the sound of his voice made him stop, something commanding, strong, immovable. Nate glanced around. They were alone.

Nate's anger changed to cold fear. The old man seemed bigger, more powerful, and not old at all.

"Come sit here," said the old man motioning to a cushion covered bench.

Nate didn't look up but kept his gaze on his shoes.

"Nate, do you remember how you got here?"

"No," Nate said in an angry whisper. "I mean, no, Sir."

"That's fine Nate, you can call me "sir," or you can call me the old man, or Ken, that's my given name, or you can call me Dad, since I am your father."

Nate looked up at the old man. "What?"

"Well, I know Joe told you, but that was in your other life so you might not remember. I adopted you Nate. Joe went out to find you, along with Alex and a few others, and brought you back here to live with us."

Nate couldn't speak. Adopted? His face was hot. His eyes inside his head were searching for a memory. He knew this was not his family. He knew he had never been here before. Nate held his head in his hands.

"Nate don't try to remember. The memories will come on their own."

"I want to remember now," said Nate.

"I know, but your mind and heart and soul can only take so much pain. Your body knows what it can handle."

Nate felt the urge to get up and run away but couldn't. The old man got up off his rocker and sat next to him on the bench, his warmth seeping into Nate. They sat like that for a long time.

Nate didn't mind.

Behind the Big House, across the lawn about a quarter mile from the party, Henry had finally finished cleaning the stalls in the front stable. The horses were sticking their heads out asking for their treat for the day.

"Not yet, Ladies," he said. "I have a celebration to go to first. I'll see you in a few hours. You too, boys."

The horses whinnied.

Henry went to his rooms which were attached to the stable. He cleaned up and changed from his work uniform to jeans, shirt, and vest. He began to whistle "I Whistle a Happy Tune." He smiled at the sound of his ladies answering back.

Outside was bright and warm. Henry found the food table and was greeted by more people than he could have ever imagined knowing in his old life. He chose lots of sides and accepted a hamburger well-done from the grill master at the end of the line.

"How are the ladies tonight, Henry?" said Chef, using his spatula to salute Henry.

"Fine, fine! You should come ride with us one of these days."

"I will," said Chef smiling an extra wide smile to go with his extra tall body. "I will do that."

Henry knew Chef would come riding the next day, and probably early in the morning. It was a tradition that had begun years ago. Chef would cook for Henry and Henry would teach Chef to ride.

They had both arrived at The Ranch on the same day. Both had come from tough, miserable lives and both had agreed to never speak of them. Henry smiled. Why ruin happiness with past pain? At that time neither knew where they would fit into The Ranch life.

"But we can't ever forget," Chef had said to Henry at the time. "That would pale our present happiness."

"True," agreed Henry.

Chef had taken to cooking right away. Henry had searched for his place for a long time, trying the things he thought he was supposed to be doing instead of waiting for the job to find him. He had escaped out the back door more times than anyone else at The Ranch, but never stayed away long. He never went back to his old life. That was too dangerous. Mostly he would hide out in the woods until he was wet and cold or until Jasper, the Seeker who had brought Henry to The Ranch, came to get him. Henry could stand being hungry. Before coming to The Ranch he had been hungry every day of his life.

Henry sat at a table with The Rest House family.

"Is that seconds or thirds?" asked Solomon, the doctor.

Henry smiled, "Just getting started, Sol. Just getting started!"

Nate and the old man came back to the party and sat with Solomon, Henry and the others. Nate was introduced all around. Nate announced his job was to sweep the hallways in The Big House. Solomon nodded and the rest of the table told Nate their jobs.

Nate was feeling better. They hadn't made fun of him for having a simple job. In fact, they made him feel like he was an equal.

"How much do I get paid?" asked Nate. Everyone was quiet for a moment. Henry was the first to speak.

"Paid? Why do you need money?" asked Henry.

"Well, you know, to buy things," said Nate.

"Well, what are you going to buy?

"I don't know, a snack or something."

"You can get a snack any time you want from Cook or one of the other kitchen staff."

"Or do what Henry does and raid the frig," said Chef.

Henry nodded. "All the things you need are here, and if you can't find them or don't know where to get them you just ask someone."

"I know, but, well, I need money."

"Why?"

"Well, in my old life I always had money in my pocket. It was something we were supposed to have, you know, just in case."

"Just in case what?"

"In case you were stranded somewhere, or you were hungry, or you needed to hire a cab or buy tissues or chips or a soda." Nate felt strange listening to his own words. Maybe he was remembering.

"I understand how you feel," said Henry. "I always had a few bucks in my pocket everywhere I went. I felt uncomfortable without it. It was like I needed money in my pocket to feel safe. It was like preparing for the weather by wearing a jacket or boots."

"That's it, exactly."

Henry paused for a while, waiting for someone else to chime in. Then he continued, "There's another problem with money. If folks know you have money, those that are bent toward stealing might take it. You wouldn't want to cause someone to steal just because you have something they want, and you don't need."

"I guess not."

"I, for one, feel much freer without having to worry about money," said Solomon. "In my old life I made pretty good money, but I always worried about it. I worried about the bank where I kept most of it. I worried that someone would find where I hid it in my house. I spent money paying for ways to keep my other money safe. So much worry."

Everyone at the table was talking about money. Some missed it, just like Nate. The old man patted him gently on the back. Nate smiled. He hadn't done anything wrong, in fact he had done something right. He had started a discussion. Somehow Nate knew that this was not something he had experienced in his old life.

Chapter 3

It was getting dark. The meal was finishing up and people began to clean the picnic area. Chef announced dessert back in the dining room. Nate and the old man walked back to the porch. The old man sat in his rocker and fixed a pipe. Nate spoke first.

"How did you know about me? I mean ... how did you know to go get me?"

"Oh, that's a long story," said the old man, "but I keep my eyes and ears open. I have lots of friends who keep me informed."

"Why would – I mean, how did Joe know – I mean ..."

"Joe is what I like to call a Seeker. You could call him a Talent Scout or a Hunter. In some circles we use the name Investigator.

"There are many Seekers who work for me. Perhaps someday you will become a Seeker as well. I think you would do well in that job. Seekers leave the ranch for a time and look for people who need a job, people who need us, who need this ranch, who need me."

Nate was quiet, thinking, trying to form a question to ask out of the thousands of muddy thoughts swirling inside his brain.

"Nate, you can come and talk to me any time you like, especially if you have questions. For now, I think you should go back for dessert. You will need your strength. You are still weak from your ordeal."

"What ordeal?"

"Let's talk about that later," said the old man rising and leading Nate to the dining room.

A new group of people were walking past the porch for the desserts prepared by Chef. As they mounted the stairs the old man was greeted with "Hi, Ken!" and "Dad!" and "Howdy, Sir." There were even some names Nate didn't understand, almost like they were in a different language.

Nate followed and chose a dessert, then found a table and sat. Nate was still hungry and ate the chocolate cream pie while listening to conversations about the cattle, the wheat, the corn, the horses, the garden, the weather, the price of sugar and fuel and lumber. It sounded as if another building was going up in another part of the ranch. Nate felt a tiny excitement growing inside of his heart. It was as if he were being welcomed as part of the family, even though no one was really talking to him. He felt safe knowing the old man was seated on the porch.

Half-way through his pie, Nate smiled.

"Hi," said Alex approaching with his ice cream sundae. He chose the one place left at the Nate's table.

"Alex!" said everyone at the table at once.

"Nate, you've met Alex," said the gentleman seated next to Nate.

Nate looked up. Alex seemed familiar, but he couldn't place where they had met.

"Yes," said Alex. "We met. Nate's been doing a great job with his first assignment."

Nate leaned in to protest. What assignment? The man whispered in his ear, "just say 'Thank you.'"

"Thank you," said Nate not sure why he was thanking Alex. He felt a bit humiliated, so he went back to eating, nibbling at the leftovers on his plate until the dark feeling went away.

After his pie was gone, he remembered – the sweeping. He had spent most of yesterday sweeping. That must be it. What a strange thing to be commended for. Everyone could sweep, right? And when had Alex seen him sweeping?

As Nate let his food digest, he felt brave enough to whisper in the man's ear, "Who is Alex?"

"Alex is the old man's son," he said with a sparkle of pride in his voice. Nate looked around. No one seemed to notice this quiet conversation. If they had heard, they were not letting on.

The sky began to turn twilight. People were cleaning up. The old man was in the kitchen washing his dishes. Nate quickly went to wash his as well.

"You should continue with your assignment," he said to Nate. "Thank you for the talk. I enjoyed it." He smiled at Nate.

"Me, too, Sir," he said.

He headed over to the janitor closet to get his broom.

He swept until his arms and back ached. The hallways seemed a little longer this time. He was tired but decided to go to the kitchen to say "good night" to Cook.

The kitchen was dark except for a light over the sink and another over the stove. No one was around. Someone stuck his head in from the dining area and said, "Kitchen's closed for the night, Nate. Snacks in the frig."

"Okay." As he made his way out of the kitchen, he passed by one of the huge silver refrigerators. Something next to the frig seemed out of place. He went over to look. It was a rifle tucked between the frig and the cabinets. Nate decided to ask Cook about that the next time he saw her – if he could muster up the courage.

Upstairs in his room he settled in his chair and wondered what to do now that it was dark outside. He got up again and opened all his draws: shirts, pants, socks, underwear, and an envelope. He pulled out the envelope. Searching in the side table drawer, he found the book, a notebook and a few pens and pencils.

Nate got comfortable in his chair again and opened the envelope. Inside was a note from Cook in graceful, delicate letters:

Nate,

The notebook and pen are for the time when you will begin to remember your old life. Write it all down.

Don't forget to read your book. It's a how-to manual about life at The Ranch and will help you in your new life here.

Breakfast will be sausage, biscuits, and gravy.

C

Nate felt that now-familiar warmth welling up in his chest. He got up, locked his door, flopped on his bed, and let the tears come. Somewhere in the back of his brain he heard stern words: "Men don't cry."

He cried anyway.

Curled up in a ball, covered in a warm blanket, he went to sleep. He dreamed of the Bar and Grill, of Joe, of Alex, and of an angry man he recognized, but could not name.

Chapter 4

A loud knocking at his door awoke Nate. The light from his window was a dim pink of the dawn breaking.

"Who is it?" he called, feeling groggy.

"It's Joe. We have to go to the meeting."

"What?" said Nate as he unlocked and opened the door.

"The meeting. I'm sorry, Nate, I forgot to tell you. I was having so much fun yesterday and it was my job to tell you. The meeting starts in 15 minutes. Can you get ready that fast?"

"Yeah, sure," said Nate. The happy serenity from the day before was gone. He blamed it on Joe. "Don't you guys have alarm clocks and stuff like that?"

"Sure, Nate. I can get you one."

"I meant you." Nate stared at Joe standing in the doorway.

"Oh, yeah," said Joe. "I'll wait in the living room, okay?"

Nate didn't answer. He just slammed the door. Somehow it felt good to be mad at Joe. But somehow the slamming made him feel even worse. He gathered his things and washed up. Today the official-looking sign said, "Bathroom," which just made Nate more irritated.

Down in the living room Nate could smell the sausage and biscuits. His stomach growled. He spotted

Joe, then turned to go to the kitchen. Joe grabbed his arm like he had the day before and said, "We don't have time to eat. C'mon!"

Nate's anger level went up another notch.

The air was brisk and Nate wished for his jacket. As they jogged through the dewy grass past The Rest House Nate tried to catch a glimpse through the front doors. Lights were on. He spotted someone behind a reception desk, but Joe was moving too fast for him to see more.

An old, three-story brownstone building hidden in the trees beyond was their destination. Nate's anger subsided into curiosity when he saw the tower.

It was warmer inside. Nate could hear singing, slow singing. Nate smacked his palm on his forehead, "Church. Really."

"Na, it's not church. That's the choir. They practice every day. Early. Do you like to sing?"

"Not really."

"Right here. Up the stairs."

The wide marble staircase curved up guided by a thick ornate stone banister. Nate imagined himself hopping on and sliding on its hard smoothness all the way down to the floor. He wished it would go up forever – that would be fun.

Joe led Nate up three flights of stairs. It seemed like the banister was continuous up to the tower. The room to which they were headed was off to the right. Nate wanted to break away from his tour guide and explore.

The third floor was one large ornate brightly lit room. Intricate tapestries warmed the brick walls leading up to the carved plaster ceiling 20 feet high. People were filing in from all directions. Joe chose a chair in the back row. This suited Nate.

The solid wood chairs were arched into semicircular rows facing a raised desk broken by an aisle. It looked a little like a courtroom, but Nate couldn't remember when he had been in a courtroom, just that he had.

Soon every seat was taken, and Alex was sitting at the desk in front. The room went quiet as he rose to speak.

"Thank you for coming. This won't take long. We need volunteers to find Miles. For those of you who do not know Miles, he is our Seeker in Arizona. He last reported from inner city Phoenix. This is not a pleasant area, but you will, of course, have security. We know where he was yesterday, but he continues to move."

The group seemed stunned by this news. Nate racked his brain for a reason why. Who were all these people and why was trying to hide such a bad thing? Isn't that what a person is supposed to do if they are tired or hurt or afraid? Maybe this Miles guy didn't want to be a Seeker anymore.

"He did find and make contact with his recruit and was in the process of giving him the information, but no decision had been reached."

The meeting was quiet for a time. Nate could hear the choir singing in the floor below. He recognized the song but caught himself before he started humming.

To Nate's right Solomon stood tall and straight. "I'll go. Who will go with me?"

"Thank you, Solomon," said Alex.

A younger man near the front of the room stood. "I'll accompany Solomon."

"Thank you, Caleb," said Alex and Solomon at the same time.

One more man, just a little older than Nate, maybe in his 20s, rose and volunteered. Then Joe stood up. Nate kept his head down not wanting to go to the desert.

Nate glanced up at Joe. His face was flushing.

"Thank you, Reuben," said Alex. "We have our Seekers: Solomon, Caleb and Reuben. You will be called Investigators. This is a very large city. Solomon, I know you have been to Phoenix. Caleb and Reuben, you will need to meet with Solomon this afternoon as he explains how things work in Arizona. You will go over maps and he will help you become familiar with the customs."

Joe sat down with a huff. His face was dark. Alex dismissed the meeting.

"I'm starving," whispered Nate. "Can we go?"

Joe had tears in his eyes. Nate pushed Joe on the arm, "Can I go?"

Joe glared at the Seekers in conversation in front of the room.

Nate slid away from Joe not knowing what else to do and went back down the stairs with the others. He forgot all about sliding down the marble banister. All he could think about was breakfast, but a tiny thought passed through his mind – the old man had said he might become a Seeker and that thought made his heart do a flip.

Chapter 5

Joe sat in the meeting room alone, occasionally wiping his eyes. He was going over the conversation he had had with Solomon the day before – over and over. What had he missed?

Solomon had told him he would be going to Arizona with a small group of Seekers. Solomon thought Joe was perfect for the assignment. Why hadn't someone told him he wasn't going before this public announcement? He was disappointed. He was humiliated. Again.

He had to walk it off. He sprung from his chair and walked up the stairs. The way to the tower twisted up another three stories.

At the top Joe watched out the window at the rear entrance to The Big House. He knew most of the people that came and went. Some were Seekers, but most were just the people that worked the ranch that wanted a snack or a word with the old man.

Being in the tower reminded Joe of Tony and another humiliation haunting him from the past. Tony was a Seeker and a jokester. Tony had convinced Joe that the tower was built especially for bad Seekers. What a fool Joe had been for believing him.

"That's where they put them when they do something wrong," Tony had said.

Joe smiled at the memory of Tony despite the

bittersweet pain. "Joey, look there!" said Tony. "See that little indentation in the grass down there? See it?"

"Yes," said Joe, who a new recruit at the time, gullible and willing to trust.

"That is where Sagus hit the ground when he fell." Tony let the news sink in to "Joey's thick skull," as he called it, and waited for the full effect.

"No way," said Joe in awe of the sacrifice of the first seeker. "Why did he jump?"

Tony paused in silence. Then he sprang the punchline, "Who said he jumped? He was running too fast and tripped over his shoelace. That's where he hit the ground. I was up here when I saw it. It was so funny! I laughed for two days!" Tony was laughing. Joe was feeling stupid and knew it wasn't true. Sagus had lived many years before either one of them had even been born.

So Joe had been terrified when later Alex had asked him to go to the tower with him one day.

They stood in front of the plaque he couldn't decipher. It was in a language that no one could translate but Alex and the old man. Sagus was The First Seeker and the plaque was a dedication to him. Alex told Joe that Sagus used to stand in the tower and look over the land and watch for people coming back to The Big House.

"There were few trees then," said Alex. "You could see all around for miles." Joe waited for Alex to pronounce some harsh judgment on him. But it never came.

Alex told Joe that Tony had gone out the back door and would never return. They had sent out many to find him and bring him home, but he had rejected the family, made fun of so many people, insulted Cook, and yelled at the old man. Joe was not surprised. He shook his head.

"Sometimes it just doesn't work out," Alex said. "Sometimes, no matter how much you love someone, they just can't accept your love. They don't trust it. They think you have some hidden evil intent. They make a conscious decision to not accept love and to be totally independent of everyone."

Then Joe asked if he could go find Tony. He was sure Tony would listen to him. Alex said that it would not be wise to do so. "To return now would be admitting he was wrong. His pride will not allow him. He will only spit in your face, as he did mine."

The memory of that conversation twisted inside Joe. He felt uncomfortable and sick. He had to think, to decide. It wasn't going to be easy. They had prevented him from going to find Tony back then. Now they had prevented him from going to find Miles.

Joe moved to the center of the room. This babysitting he had to do with Nate was just stupid.

He needed breakfast.

Back on the front porch the old man stopped Joe. "Come sit," he said.

"No," said Joe. "I haven't eaten yet. I'm hungry."

The old man looked at Joe and waited. Joe hated that. It was like the old man could read his mind.

He walked over to the old man and crossed his arms. "I don't feel like sitting."

"Are you thinking of leaving?"

Joe should have been used to the old man knowing what he was thinking, but it still irked him.

"Are you angry that you were not allowed to go to Arizona to look for Miles with the others?"

Joe pressed his lips together.

"Do not blame Solomon. Do not blame the Seekers. It was my decision to keep you here."

"But why?" Joe exploded.

"You are still angry with Tony. You still haven't forgiven the Seekers for agreeing to your personal search for him."

"But -"

"And Nate needs you."

"Oh, right. Nate. He doesn't need me. He's got Cook. He's got you. He's got Alex. He doesn't really like me anyway."

"How do you know he doesn't like you?"

"Well, he never comes to see me. He doesn't talk to me when we are together. He just seems angry with me all the time."

"Give him time," pleaded the old man. "Joe, talk to me."

That was Joe's cue to stomp into the house. He didn't want anyone's pity. The old man had made it easy for him to make his decision to leave.

Chapter 6

Nate ate breakfast in the huge dining room. Cook was creating a second breakfast for the Seekers who were filing in. Nate liked Cook and trusted her. But he wouldn't want to get on her bad side.

He washed up his dishes and went out to find Joe. He peeked into the windows of the Rest House. He searched the Brownstone Schoolhouse. He went to the red barn and at the stables he paused. He heard talking and laughing. The door opened, and two men walked out.

"Hi! You're Nate, aren't you? I've seen you around. I'm Henry!" Henry stuck out his hand and Nate instinctively took it and shook it.

"This, here, is Chef." Chef shook Nate's hand too.

"Hi, Nate," said Chef.

"Chef here is the one that cooked up those great burgers yesterday. Did you have one?"

"Yes," said Nate. "They were good."

"Good," said Chef. "You look like you could use a little more meat on your bones. I'm cooking up something special for Henry. Would you like to come with us?"

Nate thought for a moment about his quest to find Joe.

"Unless you have other plans ..."

"Oh. No, I don't have any plans."

"Good!" said Chef. "You come."

"Right this way," said Henry.

Nate followed the men through the rear entrance to the kitchen and around to the first-floor hallway. They stopped at a large, dark wooden door.

"Here we are," said Chef. He opened the door for his guests. The apartment was huge, like an entire house: a living room, a dining room, and swinging doors to the kitchen.

"It's so big!" exclaimed Nate.

"Make yourself at home," said Chef. He disappeared through the swinging doors.

Even though it was an hour since breakfast, the aroma of brewing coffee made Nate's stomach growl. Henry got comfortable in an easy chair with a magazine. Nate, feeling a little out of place, grabbed the nearest book.

Chef came out with coffee for three.

"Black for Henry," he said.

"Cream and sugar?" he asked Nate.

"Yes."

"You read French?" asked Chef.

"No. Why?" Nate had been studying the beautiful photography now looked at the words, which he could not understand. "Oh. This is French?"

The men chuckled a little.

"Well, maybe you can figure it out," said Chef rushing back to the kitchen. "Stranger things have happened."

"He means Solomon," said Henry. "He taught himself to read several languages. I think he's working on Chinese right now."

"Wow," said Nate.

Between flapping doors Nate could make out the huge kitchen, not as big as the Big House kitchen, but bigger than the one at home.

"At home" ... a wave of nausea came and went. "I think I'm remembering," he said, looking at Henry.

"You okay?" said Henry.

"I think so. That was weird."

"Did ya feel sick?"

"Yes."

"Oh, boy. Well, it will pass. Mind if I ask what the memory was?"

"I just remembered my kitchen back home."

"Back home?"

"I think so. I don't know where "back home" is."

"Well, the fact that you got sick should tell you you're in a better place."

"I guess so," said Nate.

"Hope you like fried cheese sticks!" announced Chef, bringing the aroma of fair food with him.

"Yes!" said Nate, his face brightening. A tiny, happy memory popped into his head. He was handing money to a lady in exchange for deep-fried cheese sticks at the fair. He had bought them with his own money.

After appetizers, the first course was lobster. Nate remembered lobster. There were buttered vegetables, hush puppies, deep-fried shrimp, and fresh garlic bread. The second course was baked salmon with lemon slices and baked potatoes. Henry and Nate ate on the coffee table – Henry's choice. Chef joined them.

"Dessert will be something new I just learned to make yesterday," said Chef.

They talked of riding horses and fishing, hunting and trapping, eating fresh game and camping. Nate remembered hunting and fishing, but he couldn't remember ever riding a horse. But he wanted to.

"A little wine?" asked Chef.

"Just a little," said Henry. "I'm walking home."

"None for me," said Nate, smiling.

After a little while Chef disappeared into the kitchen once more.

"Hey, Nate,' broached Henry. "You sure you weren't going somewhere when we met you at the stables?"

Nate looked down at his plate. Somehow, with Henry, he couldn't make up a fib. "Well, I was trying to find Joe. He seemed upset after the Seeker meeting this morning."

"Oh, I see. Well, when we're done maybe you should -"

"Yeah."

Henry's face brightened. "Hey, Nate! What's your guess?"

"Guess?"

"Dessert!"

"Hmmm ... I guess apple pie."

"Na. He's made that a million times. But that would be great. He makes the best apple pie and don't go tellin' Cook neither."

"Chocolate cake!" said Nate.

"Extra-large blueberry muffins!" said Henry.

A few minutes later Chef appeared with two large bowls, "Voila'! Fried ice cream! Plates are hot!"

The warm crispy fried cinnamon aroma almost made Nate cry.

Henry cut open his first. Inside the cold vanilla ice cream was not melted, and still stiff. Steam rose from his bowl.

"How did you do that?" asked Nate. "How did you get the frozen ice cream inside the hot dough?"

"Ah. It's a secret. Enjoy!"

The conversation continued with more coffee.

All too soon Henry said, "I've got chores."

"Ah, yes, all good things ..." said Chef.

"And Nate's got a job to get to, right?" said Henry.

"Right." Nate nodded but did not meet Henry's gaze.

It was late afternoon, and the kitchen staff was noisily getting dinner ready as Nate passed the kitchen.

Back in his room Nate was so stuffed he wondered if he would ever eat again. He felt sleepy and decided he would just take a nap, then go find Joe.

Nate did not nap well. He awoke several times with vivid dreams raging hot in his head. He was running and not getting anywhere. He was trying to save someone. He was treading water and getting exhausted.

Then it was early morning just before dawn with the sky glowing pink. He was completely awake and knew it was time to pull out the notebook Cook had placed on his nightstand.

Nate wrote down everything he could remember. He wrote about the angry man that slapped him in the face. He wrote about a beautiful woman that flirted with him and made him feel uncomfortable. He tried to remember the fight in the bar, but only flashes came to mind. One flash was the bartender laughing at him as if he had just done something stupid. Another flash was some large man punching him. The last picture he could remember was in the restroom looking at his bloody face in the cracked mirror.

His memories were coming back and none of them were pleasant. He hated writing but getting the images down on paper seemed to help him calm down and created the secure feeling that he wasn't going crazy. It was almost as if writing it all gave him power over the pain. And it didn't make him sick.

Voices outside his window woke him. Now the day was bright. He had fallen asleep again. His neck was stiff from dozing in the chair. His notebook and pen had fallen on the floor. Nate felt different somehow, like he belonged at the ranch. His old life was something he did not want to think about.

Just like Henry had said.

Chapter 7

Nate was hungry. He changed his clothes and went down for a late breakfast. For the first time he felt comfortable sitting at a table with other people he didn't know. He even went back for seconds.

He washed his dishes slowly, waiting for Cook to show up. Another lady was peeling potatoes this morning. She was younger and seemed nice. She said "Hi" to Nate but didn't engage him in conversation. Nate was disappointed. He really wanted to talk to Cook about writing in his notebook.

Nate swept, then went up to his room. On the way he noticed that the hallway carpet needed cleaning. He went back down to the janitor's closet on the first floor to look for a vacuum. It seemed like the closet had gotten bigger. He found it in a cubby in the closet he hadn't noticed before. He walked up the back stairs next to the closet he also hadn't noticed before and began vacuuming. Every few minutes he turned off the vacuum to listen. He was relieved no one was coming out of their rooms to say the noise was bothering them.

After his job was finished, he walked back to the kitchen. Cook was still not there. He walked up to the lady now washing pots and asked, "Where's Cook?"

"I wouldn't know, Dear. This is her day off."

Nate felt a large lump of disappointment in his chest. He really wanted to talk to her. He paced about the kitchen for a bit and looked for something to wash or put away. But the kitchen was shiny and spotless.

Then he remembered.

Joe.

Leaving the kitchen he went in search of Joe's room. He counted the doors. There were only five. He read all the signs. None of them said "Joe." He stood in the hallway hoping Joe would just appear. After a few minutes Nate gave up.

He walked to the living room and sat on a chair near the fireplace. Coals glowed in the center of the ashes.

"Go ahead," said someone behind him. Nate jumped.

"What?" said Nate, turning to see the old soldier in a chair with a book in his lap.

"Looks like you'd like to start that fire up again. That's fine by me. Go ahead."

"I'm not sure - "

"Just throw some of those small sticks in and poke around. Those coals'll catch. There's some paper over here if you need it."

Nate took some smaller sticks from a basket and threw them on. He poked at the coals with the black iron poker. In a moment he had a small flame. Then he found two fatter sticks to place on top of the smaller twigs. After a few minutes, the fire was burning as brightly as the evening before. Nate smiled and added a heavy log.

The man rose and moved to the chair closest to the fireplace. "Do you mind if I take this chair? I'm feeling a little chilled today."

"Oh, no. I don't mind," said Nate, wondrous at the thought of someone asking his permission to do anything.

"Thank you, son," said the man, putting his feet up on a stool and opening his book. "Feels good to be in The Big House again."

"Have you been on a trip?" Nate asked.

"Yep! Been buying cattle for Ken," he said.

"We have cows?" asked Nate.

"Ah, that's good a sign, son."

"What?"

"You're using the word 'we'," the man smiled at him. "That means you are accepting your position here in the family. That's good. You must be Nate."

"Yes." Nate felt a tiny wave of happiness tinged with the old familiar mistrust of new people. "How do you know me?"

"Oh, I talk to Ken a lot."

"Ken? You mean, the old -, I mean the man -"

The man laughed. "Yes, the old man on the front porch. His name is Ken, at least to us gents of a certain age. After we were here for a while and got our jobs, he insisted we call him Ken. Although, when he's giving me a job to do, I still go back to my upbringing and call him 'Sir'."

"Joe told me to call him 'Sir'."

"Good practice. So, your assignment is making fires?"

"Oh, I don't know what my assignment is. I'm still waiting for someone to tell me."

"I see. I should introduce myself. My name is Sam."

Nate walked the few steps to his chair and shook hands, surprised at his strength. "Nate," he said.

"Good to meet you, Nate."

"Pleasure to meet you, Sam." Nate returned to the fire and put another log on the flames. "How did you find out your assignment?"

"Oh, I see, you're still searching. Well, for me, I was a rowdy one. I was out the back door the very first day."

"Wow!" exclaimed Nate, taking a seat across from Sam.

"Oh, yeah. I wasn't like most that come here. I

knew my old name and my old life, and I wanted to go back real bad. But the old man said I was meant to be here, and he needed me and had jobs for me. He said I wasn't going to be any good to him if I kept running away." Sam laughed.

"You called him the old man -"

"Oh, yeah. I didn't get that at first either. When he does business, and he does a lot of business, it's 'Ken'. Some of the one's been here a long, long time, they sometimes refer to him as 'the father,' which I think is a little odd, but probably just old fashioned. When you start working for him it's 'Sir' and some around here are comfortable just calling him that. When you really get to know him, and you feel like he's your family you can call him Dad. I don't know if I'll ever call him Dad. I guess I remember my old life too much and I remember my own dad sometimes. Ken is better than a dad. He's the best boss I ever had."

They were silent for a bit.

"You said you're glad you're back. Where did you go?"

"Oh, that." Sam looked at Nate and thought. "I don't think I should tell you about where I was, not yet anyway. How long you been here?"

"I'm not sure. A couple of days, maybe. I just woke up here one day and Joe called me 'Nate' so I figured that was my name."

"Oh, I see. You haven't remembered all your old life yet. The guy I roomed with had that. Then one day he suddenly remembered. It ... well, it wasn't his best day."

"Did he leave?"

"Oh, no! He had a horrible old life. He didn't talk about it to me much, but he did spend a lot of time with the Listeners. He was different after he remembered, not so happy, but he's almost back to his old self now."

Nate felt a touch of fear. "I don't know if I want to remember everything. People are nice to me here and no one yells at me."

"Uhuh. Sounds like you're remembering without realizing it. If you appreciate the fact that no one is yelling at you here, that's a pretty good indication that people yelled at you in your old life. And if you never remember, that's okay too. I know one or two that go on the trips with me that don't remember anything and don't want to. One of them is still in the Rest House."

"Oh, the Rest House. That's the building over there, right?" said Nate pointing out a west window.

"Yup. Have you been inside yet?"

"No. Joe wouldn't tell me about it. He said someone else would."

"Hm. Well, that's okay. He might be right. Maybe it's my job," said Sam with a chuckle.

"What goes on at the Rest House?"

"Rest," said Sam with a grin. "Would you like a tour?"

"Yes!" said Nate shooting up out of his chair. Sam laughed, putting down his book. Sam rose with great effort. Nate stood ready to help and felt a little guilty about making him walk.

"It's okay. The Healers said I should be moving more. Hmm, you think that's why we met today?"

Nate shrugged his shoulders. Sam chuckled again. They walked slowly out the front door. Nate turned around and waved happily to the old man on the porch. The old man lifted a hand and smiled.

"Is he always on the porch?" asked Nate once they made it down the stairs. "Does he sleep there?"

"Oh, son, that's a hard question. I don't know. There are some that say he can be in two places at once. There are some that say they don't see him ever. Alls I knows is he's a very talented businessman and makes solid decisions based on the people he has working for him. He's creative too. I've seen him talk about new buildings and see them go up exactly as he said they would. He's got a great mind ... Without him I'd be dead.

I'm lucky to be here."

Nate noticed the stiffness in Sam's gait but didn't want to ask about it.

"Here we are – The Rest House. Nice place. Nice people. Maybe you will work here one day, you know, helping people heal."

Nate opened the door for Sam. At the reception desk the young lady smiled at them and said, "Why Sam, have you had a relapse?"

"Oh, no. Just came to give a tour for this one here. Nate, this is Jane, the front desk lady. Nicest lady you'll ever meet."

Nate extended his hand, and they shook across the desk. "Hi, Nate, welcome. I'll have to make a call first, okay?" she said.

"Sure, sure," said Sam finding a seat in the waiting area. Nate sat next to him.

Magazines and books lay on a thick rectangular shaped coffee table, calm music played from hidden speakers, and pleasant impressionistic artwork graced the walls. The lobby was big and comfortable.

There was no television, and a memory came to him of a small white waiting room with olive plastic chairs. He was watching television and waiting for someone. It was uncomfortable so he pushed it out of his mind.

"Sam, Nate, you can go in now. Solomon will give you the tour."

Solomon, a tall, solemn man, came through the door and held it open. He smiled. Nate got the feeling he was a doctor. "Hi, Sam. Hi, Nate. How are you feeling today, Sam?"

"Fine, fine. Doc, this is Nate. I wanted him to have the tour just in case. Nate, this is Doc Solomon. He does a lot of other things besides doctoring, though."

"Hi. Um ... just in case?" asked Nate.

"Just in case you should ever need us," said Solomon. His low voice created a calming inside Nate.

"Oh."

They followed Solomon.

"Sam," Nate whispered.

Sam leaned in toward Nate.

"I thought Solomon was in Arizona."

"I was," said Solomon turning around with a smile. "My two trainees are still there."

He pointed to his right and there, through a large window was a huge pool with a fountain in the middle. Lots of people were swimming on one end. On the other end there was a class going on. It wasn't like the pools Nate remembered seeing. The walls weren't some ugly color between mint and aqua. They were covered with beautiful paintings, lush landscapes, flowers, and birds – as if a skilled artist had painted paradise. Children played in the pool as well, some looked pale and wane as if getting over some sickness.

The next stop was The Movement Room. Nate expected a stale, sweaty smell, but the aroma was lemon and peppermint. The gym was filled with exercise machines, weights, mats, and tall windows with a view of the deep forest beyond, gymnastic equipment, balls and other devises Nate did not recognize. Three coaches were helping people with machines. Another man was teaching a class in martial arts.

At the end of the hallway, Nate noticed the carpet pile was high as if it had been recently vacuumed. Designs with leaves of all sorts of colors and shapes played in an organized, intricate pattern. He smelled lavender.

The mahogany door at the end of the hall opened into a dimly lit room with the aroma of pine, cedar, and a hint of spice.

"This is my favorite room," whispered Sam.

Nate closed his eyes for a count of a slow five, then opened them again just as his Aunt Betsie had taught him to do when going into a dark room. He repeated the exercise until he could see clearly. People were sitting in comfortable chairs, lounges, couches, and floor mats. Some were strapped to bars by their ankles and hanging upside down like bats. Some were lying on marble tables. Here and there were lamps emitting a rich orange glow, just enough light to navigate the room. Music played quietly; music he had heard while sweeping the downstairs hall.

"What kind of music is that?" asked Nate in a whisper.

"That is relaxation music," said Solomon. "It calms the nerves, helps the body heal, and creates an atmosphere of focus on the healing of the mind. If you can heal the mind, you can heal the body."

Nate pointed to a table near a wall filled with a few bottles and other delicate containers.

"Those are some of the herbs and oils we use in healing," whispered Solomon.

Nate felt wonderful. He wished he could crawl onto one of the couches and stay forever. He closed his eyes and-

Suddenly, Sam was pulling on Nate's sleeve. They were leaving. Nate felt as if he had been asleep. He felt energized.

Outside the door Nate asked if he could come back and stay in that room for a while.

"Only if it has been prescribed," said Solomon. "Most of us would like to sit and dream forever, but no work gets done that way. This room is only for those who have served long and hard and need to be healed from something that happened to them out in the field."

Nate looked at Sam. Sam smiled back.

They continued the tour passing windows showing offices, basketball courts, jogging areas and reading rooms.

Nate stopped to look in the windows of the library. It was decorated like the room of a castle with stone walls, floor-to-ceiling shelves, rows and rows of books, and a sliding ladder to climb to the top.

"May I check a book out of the library?" asked Nate.

"Not until you have finished reading the manual," said Solomon.

"Manual?"

"The Manual is that small blue book on your nightstand," said Sam. "It won't take you long to read, but you have to finish it before you can check out another book. Took me three weeks, but that's because I really didn't want to."

Nate felt a tiny bit of irritation in his throat. How did he know he hadn't read the book?

A distant pleasant memory of checking out books at a huge library suddenly nudged at the back of Nate's mind. The lady at the desk had asked if he could carry them all.

They passed a huge metal staircase. Nate paused. "Are we going up there?" he asked.

"That is where the private offices are," said Solomon. "You may go up there if you have an appointment with a Healer."

They had gone in a circle and arrived where they had begun. Nate and Sam said good-bye to Solomon and Jane. They walked out in the yard for a while in the general direction of the stables.

"Why can't we go to the second floor?" asked Nate.

"Have you ever been to the doctor?" asked Sam.

"I guess," Nate shrugged.

"Well, here, the offices are very private. If there is something wrong with you it isn't discussed with anyone but your doctor or healer or nurse or listener. If we went up there, we might hear something we shouldn't. You only go up there if you have an appointment. Sometimes they do surgery or other delicate procedures."

"Oh, like getting a tooth pulled?"

"Yes."

"Or getting your appendix out?"

"That's right. Sometimes the injuries are a bit more serious, but yes, that's why we don't go up those stairs."

"I see. Like a hospital."

"Yes."

After a short walk Sam said, "Nate, there's something I want to show you."

They were moving toward large red barn and stables. "Have you been around horses?" asked Sam.

"I don't remember. I don't think so."

"Well, just move slowly and don't touch them unless they invite you."

"Okay."

It was warm inside the Red Barn. The horses snuffed and neighed, stomped, and shuffled. A few stuck their heads out expecting a treat. Sam worked his way down the aisle greeting the horses he knew by name. When he got to the end stall he called softly, searching for something in his pocket. "Lady... Lady."

An old bay mare with gray hair in her forelock put her head over the stall door. "There she is," said Sam. He stroked her head and gave her some sugar cubes. He spoke to her in low tones that Nate didn't understand. It sounded like a different language.

"Lady and me, well, we've been in a few scraps, haven't we, Lady?" Sam stood by the stall and checked her eyes and ears, mouth, and neck.

"Is this your horse?" asked Nate, getting excited.

"Yes, she's mine. She came with me from my old life. The Ranch takes care of her now. Tomorrow she'll go out in the pasture and get her exercise. But we let her rest. She's done her work."

"What work did she do?" asked Nate.

"She's a warhorse, Nate. We were in The Great War together. If you go to the pasture tomorrow, you'll see her gate isn't straight. She took a bullet. But we let her run. I ride her sometimes. You should see her. Sometimes she acts like a filly! Good old Lady."

Nate was silent. There was a connection between the man and the beast that he did not understand. Nate felt afraid of horses, but he didn't want to say something stupid, so he kept his mouth shut.

"Nate, we'll go riding one of these days. You should know how to ride. You should be comfortable around horses ... and cattle, for that matter."

Nate nodded.

Chapter 8

The next day Nate woke up with a pleasant memory of watching cartoons on Saturday morning. He was relieved that it wasn't a nightmare or a bad memory. He washed and dressed and went down to breakfast. The dining room was full.

"Hi, Cook! Lots of people at breakfast today," said Nate to Cook.

"Yes, Nate, there's always lots of people," answered Cook.

"Well, when I'm here, there's usually only a few," argued Nate. "Where do they all come from?"

"They live here," said Cook. "Most times when you're here it's not a normal mealtime."

Nate couldn't quite comprehend the fact that the amount of people in the dining room did not equal the amount of people Nate had estimated during his sweeping and vacuuming hours. Maybe there was another place where people lived, like a neighborhood or an apartment complex. He grabbed a tray, filled it, and looked for a place to sit.

He sat at the last chair in a long table that seated twelve. He smiled at the rest and began eating. The conversation was mostly about cattle, horses, and fences. The women were talking about quilting and knitting and cooking and children and gardening. Nate was feeling a little like the silent child who was not given permission to speak. He finished quickly and went to wash his dishes, waiting in line to do so.

"Hey, Cook," said Nate.

"Yes, Nate."

"I wrote in my notebook yesterday."

"That's good, Nate. Did it help you feel better?"

"Yes and no. I'm starting to remember."

"Oh? In your dreams?"

"Yes, how did you know?"

"Well, I didn't. It was just a guess. That's how I remember. During the day I can think about nice things, good things, noble things. But I don't have control over my dreams."

"Do you write your dreams down?"

"Yes, when I can recall them. It helps."

Nate thought about that as he said good-bye to Cook. He wanted to talk longer, but she seemed busy.

Back in his room, he wondered about the fact that he did not recognize anyone in the dining room even though he had been meeting lots of people. He looked at the small, dusty blue book on his nightstand and thought about the huge library full of tantalizing treats. He held it in his hand and paged through it, not really paying much attention. Something inside made him feel sleepy. He tried to read the first page, then the second, but he couldn't understand much of what he was reading. It was all big words and no action. He put it down and looked through his chest of drawers to see if there was anything else to do. There wasn't unless he wanted to refold clothes.

Now he was officially bored. This was coupled with guilt because it seemed like everyone else had work to do. He didn't think he had to sweep or vacuum since the floors looked fine to him. He didn't want to bug Cook again, she seemed preoccupied. After about an hour of thinking, he got up and left his room, which had begun to feel a little cramped.

A few people were in the living room engaged in a

deep discussion. There was no fire in the fireplace, but it was too warm for a fire. Nate walked out on the porch. He looked over to the left. The old man wasn't there. This surprised Nate. A small, worried feeling grew inside his stomach as if he was forgetting something. He looked around the yard. All was quiet.

The kitchen window was open to the porch as usual, but now no sounds were coming from it. Nate felt for a moment as if he were the only one at the ranch. Everything was so quiet, eerie. There wasn't even a breeze. He sat down on the front steps and strained his ears. Nothing.

A few days ago the sound of quiet was comforting to him. Today it made him uneasy. He felt a little thought in his mind begin to form. He trotted off the steps and walked around the house. No sounds of talking or laughter.

Nate felt a deep foreboding as if he had been told about a meeting but had forgotten. Guilt moved in with the fear growing inside. He walked over to the Rest House. The doors were locked, and Jane was not at her desk.

Suddenly, the dream of Saturday morning cartoons thrust itself upon him again and he wished to be back there, wherever "there" was – some place safe. Maybe it was home. Maybe it was his Aunt Betsie's house. He sat right in the middle of the lawn between the Rest House and the Big House, placed his head in his hands and closed his eyes.

What was going on? Maybe it was his turn to go out the back door. Maybe home was better than it was here. But he didn't want to leave. He was happy here, even though he wasn't sure he fit in or that he was doing enough work. And then there was the other feeling like he was in a dream and soon he'd wake up to reality.

Suddenly, he heard cheering. It was coming from the woods on the far side of the Rest House. Relieved, he jumped up and strode toward the sound. He heard singing, beautiful singing, like a huge performing choir perfectly in tune. Maybe it was a concert or something, Nate reasoned, and since he had told Joe he didn't like to sing, maybe they didn't tell him about it.

Over to his left he could see the expansive grassy rise. A group of people was arriving. The old man was with them. He felt like he wanted to run and welcome them, but something held him back.

The group of Asian men, women, and children bowed in unison to the old man. Then there were hugs and more cheering. Nate saw Alex run from somewhere to meet them and embrace them. He felt the urge to cheer. The scene was breathtaking. And somehow in his heart he knew these new people had come from some place terrible.

Nate followed the procession into the woods, but no one seemed to notice him. They made their way toward a large bright white stone castle. Nate felt a mixture of hurt at not being noticed and awe as he listened to the old man and Alex all speaking quickly with this group in some language he didn't understand. The conversation was lively.

As he got a little closer, he was surprised to see how beat up, pale and haggard they looked. Some were dressed in rags. Nate wondered why they weren't going to the rest house first to get healed.

The trees thinned and the walls of a bright white castle rose majestic in front of them. Nate could understand some of the words to the songs now. People were dressed in white and other bright colors, hanging out of the castle windows, and standing along the castle walls calling, and waving. They didn't seem to see him either. Maybe it was a wedding, he thought.

Nate felt a wave of something deep inside; something important was happening.

On a balcony at the top of the white castle's front wall were men dressed up in costumes from all over the world, cheering, yelling, calling out things in different languages, saying chants and singing songs. Some were dancing, waving multicolored flags and branches of different kinds of trees. It was as if Nate were watching a play, but it felt real.

Nate followed as they entered the castle through the huge open doors. The cheering outside faded to an echo. The light was dim in the large open room, but his eyes grew accustomed to it. Sunshine came from high windows, candles graced tables and lit torches branched out from the walls. The room was comfortable and warm.

They walked into another larger, brighter room, the ceilings still higher. A raised pool stood in the middle of the room, large and inviting. Beautiful tapestries hung on the walls, long and ornate, in blue, purple and red. A golden thread wove back and forth throughout the pieces to create an intricate diamond pattern. Three-foot long tassels clung to the bottom of the large rug-thick masterpieces.

The voices became subdued as in special reverence. Quietness echoed in the room signaling the ceremony. Streams of sunlight color played along the floor and the walls. Nate looked up to see colorful stain glass windows with pictures displayed in them.

Suddenly, he felt odd and out of place. No one had told him about this place. Maybe it was secret. He couldn't imagine how rich the old man was to be able to afford to build this crazy castle with all the strange people that seemed to live here. And, he thought to himself, they are all happy. Very happy. Celebrating happy.

Some of the group walked a few at a time into the pool. Some were gaunt, as if they were about to die. The pool swirled with red. Nate thought, maybe the red was a special herb or medicine. Maybe the pool had special lighting. Some of the people were bleeding as they entered the pool. Maybe this is a different kind of healing place, one for those with a special kind of sickness.

As each one walked out of the pool, they were changed, completely clean, healed, and naked. Nate felt a little embarrassed. He watched as Alex and the old man wrapped a bright white bathrobe around each one. Nate was shocked that one small girl was missing an arm going into the pool, but when she came out it had been restored. After she put on her robe she began giggling and dancing. The little girl's display of happiness made Nate want to cry.

Nate suddenly wanted to hide until the room was empty and go into the pool himself. It must hold special medicine indeed. Maybe his aches and pains would go away. Maybe he would have more energy. Maybe the hurt in his heart would go away, too, and he could be truly happy like that little girl.

Then fear gripped Nate. The reality of what he was seeing did not fit with the reality of the world he thought he was part of. Maybe he was dreaming. But this didn't feel like a dream. He pinched himself until it hurt. He felt compelled leave, run away. He felt like something bad would happen if he stayed.

A group of brightly dressed people from another part of the castle came to hug and welcome them. They led the freshly cleansed group to a room far off to the right. The group entered a huge dining room for a feast, one in which Nate could not participate. He heard music, laughter, the clattering of dishes and singing coming from the next room. He smelled the aromas of a wonderful feast. It seemed logical in a way since they had arrived beaten up and starving.

Nate ran back to the entry room. He had to leave.

Suddenly, Alex was beside him.

"Are you feeling okay?" asked Alex.

"Oh! Alex... No. I feel a little sick. Who are those people? Why couldn't they see me? Why are you the only one who's talking to me?"

"They were prevented from seeing you," said Alex, leading Nate out of the castle. "They have come home for the last time. This is where they will be staying now. They have served a long time and earned their rest."

"Like being retired?"

"Yes," said Alex

"But the children -"

"Yes, they are retired, too."

"I feel like I'm dreaming," said Nate.

"I guess in a way you are dreaming," said Alex. "Maybe a better word for it would be having a vision."

The words "a vision" frightened Nate. He was quiet as they walked through the woods. Maybe it was something I ate, he thought.

"No," laughed Alex, "it isn't anything you ate."

Nate felt a flip in his stomach. How did Alex know what he was thinking?

"Is it like a vision of the future?" Nate asked.

"Something like that," said Alex. "Give yourself some time. Soon you will understand."

Back at the big house Alex walked back toward the castle and Nate walked up the porch steps. He noticed there were people on the porch talking to the old man. Nate wondered how the old man could be on the porch when he had just seen him at the castle. He was afraid to ask and went into the kitchen instead.

Cook was putting bread into the oven to bake.

"I saw the castle," Nate blurted out.

Cook put a finger to her lips and looked around the kitchen. She wiped her hands on her apron and whispered, "We better go talk in my room." She gave instructions about the bread to another kitchen helper and led Nate down the first-floor hallway.

As they entered Cook's room Nate caught the aroma of cinnamon and some other spice he didn't recognize. The large room was brightly decorated with masks, wood carvings, animal skins, paintings on the walls and sculptures on the tables.

Cook sat down. Nate sat as well. Cook took a deep breath and thought for a moment.

"Not many get to see the castle," said Cook. "We don't talk about it around the new people."

"Why?" asked Nate.

"Once in a while a new person will hear about it and go try to find it. They always get lost in the woods."

"I didn't get lost."

"Alex was with you, right?"

"Yes, how did you know?"

"Child, you are so fortunate, but you need to wake up. If Alex allowed you to follow, you were meant to see. Did you see someone come over the knoll?"

"Yes, a whole group of people."

"Oh, how wonderful," said Cook looking up toward the ceiling, small tears forming in her eyes. "I'm a bit envious. Did you see the father greet them?"

"Yes, the old man and Alex both went out to see them. The people were all beat up like they had been in a fight." Nate was getting excited as he remembered.

"Oh, Child, you are special. You are chosen. Very few of us have seen that castle and those rooms. Most of the folks in this house haven't even heard about it."

"Can you see it?"

"Yes, I can."

"Have you seen the huge rooms in there? And the pool?"

Cook pressed her lips together and closed her eyes. Then after a pause she said, "No, but some have told me about it and that's just fine with me. I know it's there and I know what it's for. It gives me a deep comfort inside. I am content." Cook opened her eyes and smiled.

"What's it for? What were they doing in there?"

"I'm sorry, Child," said Cook. "I cannot tell you that. Only Alex can tell you. You will have to ask him."

Nate felt irritated. "Why do they keep so much a secret? Why can't everyone know about everything? Why do they keep so much from us? Don't they trust us?"

"Don't you trust Alex? Don't you trust the old man?"

Nate shrugged.

Cook got up and walked to her kitchen. She came back with a soft drink in a silver glass. Nate took it.

"Manners, Honey," said Cook. "Even when you are upset, mind your manners."

"Thank you," said Nate.

"You're welcome."

After a few minutes, Nate put down his drink. Cook sat next to him, took his face in her large warm hands, and looked him in the eyes.

"You haven't been reading your book, have you?"

Nate tried to look someplace else. How did she know?

"Well?"

Nate couldn't meet her gaze.

"Okay," said Cook firmly. "Here's what we are going to do. You go back to your room right now and read the first chapter all the way through. Then come find me and ask me a question about it."

"But -"

"Go now, Child. This is very important. You need to be reading that book. Especially after what you've just seen."

"Okay," said Nate getting up and walking to the apartment door.

"Manners?"

"Oh," said Nate. "Thank you for the drink, Cook."

"You're welcome, Honey. Have a good evening."

"Bye," said Nate in a whisper.

"Good-bye, Nate, thank you for coming."

Nate shut the door behind him.

Feeling hurt and humiliated Nate went to his room and stared at the dusty blue book. He flipped through it. Now it seemed big and heavy and boring. He let it flop on the bed.

Cook was right – more than right. He hadn't read his manual at all. He shut his eyes and said a short prayer to no-one-in-particular. He found the first chapter and paged through it to see how long it was. He was pleasantly surprised to see that it was only three pages long. Nate flipped the chapter back and forth to make sure no pages were stuck together.

Yup. Three pages.

Nate turned the light on that was over his bed that he hadn't noticed before and began reading. The words were easy to understand. The thoughts expressed made sense to him. In fact, Nate found the book interesting. At the end of the chapter he closed the book and tried to think of a question for Cook. He couldn't. A tiny light of success grew in his chest. He couldn't remember ever reading anything that made him feel smart. Not even in school.

Nate opened the book again and turned to the second chapter. He kept reading until he fell into a peaceful sleep, the book nestled on his chest.

Chapter 9

The next day Nate started his day with an early morning walk. The old man greeted him on the front porch with a wave. Nate opened the screen door but stopped right inside and listened. A light breeze seemed to be pushing him inside, but he stayed. The old man was talking to someone. Nate couldn't see anyone else on the porch. Strange. Where was the person the old man was talking to?

While washing up from breakfast, Nate asked Cook about what he saw, or rather, what he didn't see.

"Child, you sure are getting the crash course of this place," said Cook, laughing. "Sometimes there are lots of people on the porch with Ken, but you can only see one, or two. Sometimes, like I said before, it seems like the old man is in more than one place at the same time. I don't know why. I don't try to understand it. I'm just happy to be living here with my family and my friends. I have a place to sleep. I have clothes to wear. I have plenty of food to eat. I'm doing something every day that I love to do, and I get days off if I need them. I think it's best to leave questions unanswered sometimes."

Nate felt like he had been reprimanded. He knew he could ask questions, so he decided to ask Joe the next time he saw him.

Nate walked to Joe's room on the first floor. Now

there was a sixth door. He knocked. There was no answer and no sound coming from the room. He knocked louder and placed his ear to the door, listening. He really wanted to talk to Joe. He hadn't seen him in days, and he had so many questions.

No answer. Then thought of Henry. Maybe Henry knew about the invisible people.

At the stables Nate found Henry busy clearing out stalls.

"I just saw something I don't understand," said Nate.

Henry laughed. "I see that just about every day of my life!"

"I was wondering if you could explain it to me -"

"Well, I'd love to talk, but I have work to do. Of course, if you'd like to help me, I could get done faster. Then we could talk."

"Sure," said Nate.

Ten minutes later he was sorry he had agreed. Clearing out stalls was not like sweeping or vacuuming. The only redeeming quality to the job was laying down the clean fragrant straw when the stall was cleaned. It was two hours before they were finished. Then the horses needed to be fed and watered. Nate complained. Henry explained the horses needed to be fed three times a day unless they were out in the pasture.

Nate was hungry and Henry suggested they talk during lunch.

After washing up Henry said, "You did a good job today, Nate, especially for your first day."

"Thank you. I think I'll go back to sweeping."

Henry chuckled.

They walked into the dining room together. Lunch was lasagna and salad and corn and mashed potatoes. Nate's stomach groaned in response to the spicy smell. They chose a table in the corner and after the food was dispatched, Nate asked all his questions.

"Well, that's a lot of questions," said Henry,

laughing. "I guess I don't think so much about things like you do. As far as who was on the porch with Ken and not being able to see who he's talking to, I wonder if maybe the person he was talking to was in front of the porch or maybe off to the side in the yard ... or even behind a tree. There's plenty of places a person can stand and be hidden from someone peeking out the front door. And I guess, now that you mention it, it does seem like Ken is in more than one place at the same time. But I guess he has to be. This is a huge operation.

"As far as the castle, I haven't heard of it, but I believe you saw what you saw. If Alex was there talking you through it, I'd just keep it between you two and ask him. I know this ranch is bigger than anyone can measure, and I know Ken has business ventures in just about every country in the world. He's up on all the wars and rumors of wars and genocides and turf fights and refugee movements. We have refugees living here if you didn't already know that."

"Really?"

"Yes," said Henry. "You know Solomon is a refugee."

"No. Wow. I couldn't tell," said Nate.

"Well, I don't know how you could tell," Henry said, his voice low. "I think they would have to tell you. Solomon was beat up when he got here, emaciated with hunger and wounds that weren't healing properly. After he got healed up, he begged Ken to let him work at the Rest House healing others."

Nate was silent, thinking. Maybe he didn't need to be asking all his questions. Maybe somethings were supposed to be the way they were, and the reasons weren't important. Maybe the answers would come on their own in time.

Nate changed the subject. "How long have you been here?"

"Ha! That's a good question," said Henry. "I don't know. It seems like years and years, but then, some days, when the memories of my old life come a' hauntin' me, it seems like just yesterday that I got here. If you haven't already noticed, not many talk about their age or how long they've been here. No one keeps track of time much unless there's a meeting they have to go to. Ken likes the Navajo way of thinking: There's sun-up and there's sun-down and there's the middle of the day. If there's to be a meeting, after breakfast is a good time. You don't need to spend a lot of time in meetings if everyone knows what they are supposed to do and if everyone does their own work.

"That's not to say we don't help each other. You helped me today. That was enjoyable. But the stable is my job, and not yours. You can help if you want, but you aren't responsible. That's the way it should be. I'm not the only one helping with the stables, there are others, and I get days off when I want them, and sometimes I get sick, and others come and help. No guilt. No pressure. Just do your best."

Nate was smiling. He liked the way things were run at the ranch. Everyone he met seemed to like what they were doing. He liked sweeping, but he wanted more. He told Henry so.

"Well, you talk to the old man about that. He'll find you something. He knows folks pretty well and knows how much they can handle. Some folks can't handle much. Some need lots of jobs to keep busy. You ask him, okay?"

"Sure. Thanks, Henry."

Nate left to do the sweeping. He thought he would be tired after working the stalls, but instead he was invigorated and ready for more.

Afterwards he decided to go listen to the choir sing. He explored around the outside of the brownstone building. The tower was visible from all sides. There were turrets and gargoyle waterspouts and spaces that looked like castle walls and balconies. Nate walked up the steps and into the building. As he stood in the entrance looking away from the marble staircase and to the right, he felt as if he had been there before, a long time ago. He heard a voice speaking.

Nate moved in the direction of the sound of the man's voice. Down the hallway to the right he found the room. The door was open and there were children sitting in desks. Nate quickly moved away from the room, worried that he might distract the class. He went back to the marble staircase and sat. He had been in this building before; not the Seeker meeting, but a long time ago. He was sure this was his old school room. He remembered sitting at just such a desk, desperately trying to stay awake so that he wouldn't be embarrassed by the teacher yet again.

Nate was filled with a large sadness. He could feel the distant fear he had felt when walking to school, knowing at any time he could fall asleep because he had not slept well the night before. He smelled his sour clothes and got a glimpse of his torn-up tennis shoes.

Nate closed his eyes and tried to remember more. He was suddenly very tired. The bell ringing jerked him awake. Children walked past him, talking and laughing. They smiled at him and said "Hello" as they passed, perfectly accepting of his presence in their school. Nate got up and walked to the classroom. He tentatively stepped inside.

"Why, Hello there. Can I help you?" came a tenor voice.

"Hi," said Nate. "I didn't know there was a school here."

"Oh, yes. We have four classrooms. Lots of learning going on. All first floor, you understand. They aren't allowed in the upper floors. Second floor offices. Third floor meeting room."

"Yes, I know about the meeting room," said Nate.

"Have you attended a meeting, then?" asked the teacher.

"Yes. Just a few days ago. About Seekers going to

Arizona."

"Oh, yes, I heard about that."

"Oh, right," said Nate. Maybe that would be where Joe was, he thought, Arizona. "I was wondering about Joe, since I hadn't seen him for a while."

"Joe?"

"Joe, the Seeker."

"Hmm. I don't think I know him. Sorry. But you are welcome to check the rest of the rooms."

"That's okay. Well, I better be going. I'll go check his room again. Nice meeting you -" Nate stuck out his hand - "I'm Nate."

"Hi, Nate. My name is Craig. The students call me Mr. Craig."

"Mr. Craig."

Nate jogged back to the Big House with a struggle forming in his mind. Joe had always told him to come and see him. He had even made him feel guilty because he didn't. And then, when he wanted to talk to Joe, he couldn't find him.

Nate went back to Joe's room and knocked. Someone opened the door. It was Alex.

"Oh, Hi, Alex," said Nate. "I was looking for Joe."

Alex looked sad, in fact, Nate couldn't remember seeing anyone look sad at the ranch, much less Alex, who was always happy and encouraging. A small ball of worry started winding up in Nate's stomach.

"Come in Nate," said Alex. "There is something you should see."

Nate suddenly wanted to give an excuse to leave. Something was wrong. He didn't want to deal with it. He froze. His face got hot. His head felt fuzzy.

Alex gently led Nate into the room. He handed Nate an envelope with no writing on is and sealed with wax.

"This was meant for you," said Alex.

Nate sat on the bed and felt like he might cry. He looked around the room and noticed how stark it was from the rest of the rooms he had been in. No art or posters on the walls. No books or other things to occupy free time. Why had Joe kept his room like this? It felt like the old run-down hotel room he had stayed in when-

A dark memory of being sick and alone crawled into the front of his mind. He had done something bad. He squelched the memory, squeezing his eyes shut.

He opened the envelope. The letter was written in a childish scrawl, barely readable:

Dear Nate,

Thanks for being my friend. I don't have many friends at the ranch and I really didn't fit in there. I tried really hard to fit in. I even got trained as a seeker, and a healer - I bet you didn't know that - and I even tried my hand as a letter writer. Nothing seemed to fit. Nothing was good enough.

I brought you to the ranch because the old man told me I had to. I didn't want to. I didn't want to give you the tour and I didn't want to have to watch over you like a baby. I don't know why the old man asked me. After we got back, I realized I just wasn't ranch material. I was done trying. It was time to go back to my old life, my old family, and my old job. I liked my old job. Tony was the seeker that came to get me. He wasn't ranch material either. He didn't know what he was doing. I'm sure he got me mixed up with someone else.

But you don't know the story, do you? I was working as a waiter in the upscale restaurant in Chicago called Clyde's. I got lots of tips and all the free pasta I could eat. I lived in a small third-floor apartment down the street, so I walked to work. It was a nice life. I had a small bundle saved up and I was going to go on a trip when I earned my first two-week vacation.

But Tony showed up and started talking to me about my life and asked if I was happy. He didn't believe me when I said I was. He kept showing up every few days until my boss took me aside and asked who the guy was. I told him I didn't know. He said I'd be fired if the guy kept bugging everyone.

He showed up again and I told him to leave. Then I pretended he wasn't there. I just ignored him. My boss spotted him out on the street in front of the restaurant and that was it. I tried to explain about the weirdness of this Tony guy, but my boss was mad and wouldn't listen. So, I was out of a job.

The handwriting was now reduced to hen scratching, but somehow Nate could hear Joe's voice speaking to him as he looked at the words.

Tony showed up the next day at my apartment with some other guy. I think it was Alex. The next thing I knew, I was laying in my bed here at the ranch. Tony took me around and then pawned me off on Solomon. Pretty soon I hear Tony was kicked out because of his playing pranks on the newbies. So there I was – stuck.

"*So, I fit in as best I could, got trained, like I told you, tried a bunch of jobs the last of which was seeker. Then the old man told me to go to New York to get you.*

"*I am so out of here. Good luck. You're gonna need it! - Joe*"

Nate put the note down. He remembered his own hotel room after he ran away from home. He remembered eating bread and jelly. He remembered the bar in the city where he worked. He felt sick.

"Would you like to keep it?" asked Alex.

"No," he handed it back to Alex. Why should he keep a letter that blamed him for everything bad?

"Well, why don't you keep it in your room for a while, just in case you would like to read it again."

"Don't you need it, like, I don't know, for the family or something? Isn't there someone else he was really good friends with?" asked Nate.

"Joe didn't die, Nate. He just went back to his old life. Everyone here has that freedom. We don't want you to stay if you are unhappy here."

Nate thought for a moment. Alex waited. He

wasn't impatient with him. He didn't pace. He didn't push him to make up his mind quickly. He just sat there and waited for Nate to decide what to do.

"Who gets his room?" asked Nate looking around.

"No one," said Alex. "Once you have a room here at the ranch, you have that room forever. You can come back any time you like."

"But through the front door, right?" Nate said to his feet.

"Right," Alex smiled.

Nate looked around one last time and then got up to leave.

"Nate," said Alex, pressing the envelope into Nate's hand. "Joe didn't have the old life that he described in the letter. That letter was written out of bitterness and anger."

"Why are you telling me this? I didn't really know him that well."

"Because soon you might want to go and find him. I want you to know what you might be getting yourself into. His part of Chicago was pretty rough, and he was working with evil people. Even if he gets his old job back, he's walking back into an environment that will eventually kill him. You can't convince him to come back. That decision is entirely his."

Nate shrugged. It bothered him that Alex thought he could read his mind or tell him his future. It irritated him that Alex knew what the letter said without reading it. Why would he want to leave the ranch just because Joe left? He liked it here. For the first time Nate was thinking that Alex was wrong.

Nate went back to his room and stuffed the note at the bottom of one of his drawers. Somehow the ranch seemed a little smaller without Joe. Nate couldn't figure out why that would be. He and Joe hadn't spent that much time together. It wasn't as if they were close friends or anything. It's just a place, he thought, a place where he lives, a place where he works, a place that apparently saved him from a bad life ... whatever that meant.

Nate lay on his bed and stared up at the ceiling thinking about his old life. He knew he had gone to school in a school building just like the one on the ranch. He knew he woke up Saturday mornings to watch cartoons. He knew he had lived in New York and worked at a bar. He knew he had lived in a dumpy hotel room. He also wondered, deep down inside, if something bad had happened in his family. He couldn't remember his mother or his father. Did he have a sister or a brother?

It seemed strange that he was adopted, but no one at the ranch seemed to know ... or care ... or ask. It didn't make sense that Joe would say he was there to help him and then leave. Nate had lived on his own, but here he felt as if he was being treated like a child. Most of the time he didn't mind, but sometimes, just for a few minutes, he wanted to be treated like an adult.

Why don't they tell me everything? Nate thought. Lay it all out on the table. Let me make up my own mind whether I want to stay or go?

He felt his mind getting fuzzy. He couldn't think straight. He was confused. He closed his eyes and felt very much alone. Then he fell asleep.

Chapter 10

Nate awoke with a start. How long had he been asleep?

He opened the door. It was Sam and Henry.

"Greetings, Nate."

"Howdy, Nate."

"Hi," said Nate, still a little groggy. "You guys know each other?"

"Oh, yeah," said Sam. "Go way back."

Henry laughed. "Back further than I'd like to admit." Sam smiled.

Their attitude was contagious, and Nate smiled back, his previous musings forgotten.

"Heard your friend left out the back door," said Henry. "We came to cheer you up."

"He's not my friend," said Nate.

"Anyone that brings you here is your friend," said Henry.

Nate shrugged.

"But no matter," said Sam. "We want to show you the New Building."

Sam and Henry looked so excited; Nate couldn't resist being just a little excited too.

As they passed through the kitchen Cook handed each of them a paper bag lunch.

Nate felt butterflies in his stomach as they arrived at the stables.

"Nate, this is Kane. Kane, Nate. Give him a pat and talk to him," said Sam.

Nate couldn't remember ever talking to an animal. He felt silly. He tried to think of things that someone tells a horse but ended up pleading with the animal not to kill him. Henry exploded with laughter and Nate could feel a flinch in Kane. Nate whispered calming words to Kane.

Up on the horse that seemed way too tall, Nate felt a different feeling altogether. He couldn't name it. But it was good, almost like being grown up – and floating mid-air.

They rode north beyond the stables, past the Rest House, the brownstone, and the woods, and out into open pasture. They went through a gate, Sam expertly opening and closing it without leaving his seat on his war horse, Lady, who tossed her head and snorted in anticipation as if she were young again.

They rode over a ridge revealing a lush, gentle slope into a valley, rows of tended plants and fruit trees. The aroma evoked a memory in Nate of weeding a tiny garden. It was a good memory.

They rode past raised beds full of vegetables tended by gardeners weeding and watering. Nate recognized peppers, onions, tomatoes, and the giant leaves of the pumpkin, squash, and rhubarb. Beyond the tended raised beds were fruit trees: peach, apple, and pear. Workers waved and shouted at Henry as they picked fruit and pruned.

Henry shouted a greeting and waved. Turning to Nate he said, "I work in the orchards sometimes. Keeps me young."

Sam was nodding his head. "I hope to be well enough to help with the apples. Can't wait for the cider time!"

"Apple pie!" chimed Henry.

The path they road north was wide, and the vast gardens spread out to the east and to the west.

Nate was amazed how the gardens went on and on. Beyond the many colors of apples, reds, greens, and deep purples, were fruit trees new to Nate.

"What's this?" he asked Sam.

"Hawthorne. You can tell by the thorns. Five inches long, some of them. The haws are used for jelly and juice. I hear the healers use them too. Over there are rose bushes. The Healers use the rose hips for tea and medicine. Some of those rose bushes are as big as trees at the base of the trunk."

The aromas of rose mingled with spice floated up to Nate.

The hill continued to descend gently. The fragrance seemed to work its way into Nate's very soul.

"I love this part of the ride!" yelled Henry. "Herbs and spices!"

"Herbs?" asked Nate.

"Yes," said Henry. "You know, oregano, basil, garlic, rosemary, thyme – the stuff you put in spaghetti sauce and lasagna."

Henry stopped and dismounted.

Nate struggled off his horse, trying to do it like the men, but his shoe got stuck in the stirrup. He ended up sliding down the side of the saddle and landing hard on the ground. At least I didn't fall off, he thought.

The men made no comment. Nate was thankful for that. He was already stiff as he marched in place to get his legs to work again.

"Come over here," said Henry, standing by an herb bed. Nate obeyed. Henry broke off a leaf from a small spreading plant with dark green leaves. "Close your eyes and smell this."

Nate sniffed timidly. "Oregano."

"Right."

Sam showed him his favorites. Some smelled terrible to Nate. Others brought back memories of wonderful foods. A pleasant memory of clipping tiny leaves made Nate smile.

"Maybe they'd let me garden too," chimed Nate.

"Maybe. This ranch produces everything you'd ever need," said Henry. "Vegetables, fruit, wheat, corn, oats, eggs, chickens, cattle, cheese, goats, sheep, wool ... everything."

"Even maple syrup!" said Sam. "Hey, Nate, we have to make tracks so we can get to the north base of the valley and back before dark," said Sam sounding like an army commander.

"Yes, Sir." Nate struggled back on his horse.

Past the gardens the trail changed. The terrain became rocky and wild like a desert. The air was warmer and drier. Nate spotted a lizard scampering on the rocks.

"Hang on to your saddle, there, Nate," called Henry. "We don't want to lose you if Kane spots a snake or something else that spooks him."

Fear flashed inside Nate. He readjusted his grip on the saddle horn, rewrapped the reigns around his hand, and gripped the sides of Kane with his legs. They were descending sharply. The horse swayed right and left. Nate tried to relax, but his legs and stomach muscles were sore.

Henry said, "We'll stretch our legs a bit when we get to the bottom." It seemed like a long ride to Nate, but it didn't seem like the sun had moved.

At the bottom a picnic area had been cleared out from rocks and shrubs. Nate sat at a table. Henry unpacked the lunches. Sam led the horses through the brush for a drink. A pleasant memory of a family picnic worked its way to the surface inside Nate's head. Then Henry grinned, pulled out a can of soda and handed it to Nate.

Nate smiled, "My favorite."

Henry nodded.

"Henry notices things," said Sam. "Not like me. I'm usually clueless."

"That's not true. Sam, here, can spot trouble

miles away. He can smell it on the wind. He's helped us out a time or two when the enemy was causing trouble."

Sam cleared his throat.

"Oh," said Henry. "I don't know if we're supposed to talk about that yet, but I think you should know. We get trouble occasionally."

Sam remained silent.

"What kind of trouble?" asked Nate.

"There's a guy wants the ranch," said Henry. "Sometimes when the weather is bad, we don't hear from him or see his minions for months. But when the weather is good, it's like he's got nothing better to do than terrorize us at the borders or send in spies to spread lies to the newbies or steal cattle – as if they need more than they already have. Sometimes they even steal some of our employees away by offering them lots of money."

"What do we need money for," said Sam. "We have everything we need right here."

Nate nodded. "I wondered where my money went. But I haven't missed it at all … or my phone for that matter."

"Yeah, who needs phones," said Henry. "I haven't used a phone for years. Well, some folks, even when they have everything they need, still want more."

"Greed," said Sam.

"Yup. And pride. Like they want to be a part of something bigger than this," said Henry.

"Bigger? Than this ranch?" asked Nate.

The men were silent for a minute, looking at each other.

"Can we trust him, you think?" asked Sam.

"Maybe," said Henry. "Let me go talk to Ken."

Sam nodded.

"Trust me with what?" said Nate sitting up straight. Maybe he was getting a new job.

Henry walked away from the picnic area, taking his sandwich with him, and disappeared behind a large outcropping of rock.

"I thought Henry didn't have a phone," whispered Nate, suddenly wanting to take the words back.

"He doesn't," said Sam. "There's lots of ways to communicate with people besides phones. Phones are just easier, so people get dependent on them. For example, when was the last time you wrote a letter?"

Nate thought for a bit. "I don't think I ever have."

"You never wrote a letter? Not even to your parents when you were away at camp or to some far-away relative that wanted to hear from you? Or a pen pal from another country?"

Nate thought about it, then he felt a humiliated. "I don't remember."

"Well, son, that's okay. I don't claim to be the best letter writer myself. I used to write to my mom and my sweetheart when I was in the army. They always answered my letters, even though sometimes it took weeks to arrive because we moved around so much."

"Where were you in the army?"

"In other countries. I don't like talking about it. It makes me remember. Sometimes I don't like remembering the things I remember, you know?"

"Yeah. Like me today," said Nate.

"Like today?"

"Well, I was in the meeting building – there's a school there – and -"

Nate stopped talking. He moved his head in the direction of the sound.

"That's the river," said Sam standing. He motioned for Nate to follow him.

They walked a few hundred yards in the opposite direction of where Henry had gone, down a gentle incline, through rocks and brush. They moved through a crop of trees and suddenly, there it was.

The river moved quietly, wide, and deep. The water glistened in the sun as it moved like velvet in a breeze. The horses moved toward them thinking it was time to go.

A man standing on the opposite shore waved at Sam who waved back. Neither spoke for the man was fishing.

The gliding waters of the river drew Nate into a calm state of awareness. It seemed as if each molecule of water vibrated with life, as if at any moment a new and beautiful creature never seen would emerge, fresh and clean.

"Take a drink," whispered Sam.

Nate stooped down and cupped the water in his hands. Kane walked over to join him. The water was cool and sweet. Nate felt a warm glow growing inside and he took another drink, this time splashing water on his face and neck. He noticed the soreness in his legs and back were gone.

"Where does it go?" asked Nate, working the geography out in his head.

"Don't know. Runs forever, I'd say. Never known it to dry up."

"Can we take some with us?" whispered Nate.

"Maybe on the way back," said Sam. We should get going." Sam waved again to the fisherman and started back up the rise. Nate took a last drink at the river.

Henry sitting at the picnic table. "It's fine," he said.

Sam nodded to Henry. "You were saying about the school, Nate?"

"What about the school?" asked Henry.

"He had some kind of bad memory," said Sam.

"Yeah," said Nate, suddenly not wanting to share. "I remembered being really scared at school. In fact, I thought the schoolhouse was the school I went to. It was weird. I almost passed out."

"Hmm," said Henry. "Sounds like you might have some bad feelings when all your memory comes back. You might even get sick."

"Henry, don't scare the boy," said Sam.

"Well, I think he should be ready, don't you?" said Henry.

"I'm not a boy," muttered Nate.

"No, you're not," said Sam. "You're ready for what's ahead."

"Sure," said Henry. "Okay. Ken gave the go-ahead." Sam nodded to Henry.

"Nate," Henry began, taking a seat across from him at the picnic table, brushing dust and leaves away in preparation. "We have an enemy. Well, actually, several enemies, but the one big fish is the one you should know about."

"Okay," said Nate.

"His name is Phil Amor and he's got more land, more buildings, more crops, more people, more resources, more cattle, more money, more gardens, more finery, and more connections than we have at this ranch. He's got most of the power and influence in this part of the country. And he wants more."

"Yup," Sam chimed in. "It's like a game to him."

"In the past he used to just raid our outlying camps. Now he sends in trained spies. He recruits from the inside, those that go out the back door, so that when they come back -"

"- and are welcomed with open arms -" added Sam.

"- they act as spies and give away our weaknesses and our locations to the enemy, they sabotage our get-togethers and our barn-raisings – things like that."

"That's why you need to see the New Building that everyone is so excited about," said Sam. "You will be called upon to protect it someday."

"You mean, be a guard?" asked Nate, feeling a mixture of pride and excitement.

"Yes," both men said together.

"That plan that the enemy has," said Nate thoughtfully, "... it doesn't make sense."

"Since when does evil make sense?" said Henry.

"And letting them come back just so they can sabotage again ... it doesn't make sense either."

"It's called forgiveness," said Henry quietly.

"Done eating?" interrupted Sam. "We have to get a move-on."

They mounted and descended to the path along the river. A large glass building nestled between the rocks came into view. As they drew near a greenhouse every bit as tall as the Big House rose high above them. Nate could see trees inside, palm trees, citrus trees, and banana trees. Through the misty windows he could hear music and see people working among the rows of plants.

Past the greenhouse the twisting path was choked with wild brush. Nate looked back from where they had come. The greenhouse was hidden.

Nate could hear voices, hammering and heavy machinery. It made him feel proud and just a little older.

They came out of a copse of low scrub trees along the riverbed and emerged into an open area full of construction. Trucks, bulldozers, jeeps, trailers, tents, stacks of bright lumber and shiny steel lay in neat piles everywhere. Nate counted 30-plus men working, laughing, joking, sweating. Nate wanted to jump down and help. Kane felt his excitement and pranced. Nate leaned over and patted him on the neck.

Sam led them to where the other horses were picketed. Dismounting, they were greeted by a large gray-haired man.

"Sam! Henry! Come to help?" he said.

"Sorry, Pete, just a visit today," said Henry. "This here's our newest, Nate."

Nate shook hands with Pete whose hand completely enveloped his own. It was rough and strong and warm. Something inside Nate sparked a memory. He pushed it away for later.

"Welcome, Nate. We're raising the south wall if

you want to watch," said Pete.

"Sure," said Nate following him. Nate saw a flash of memory that momentarily blotted out his view of the uneven ground. A large, greasy hand demanding his money – the landlord.

Joyous, focused yelling drew Nate's gaze back to the new building. Twelve men grabbed the top of the wall and walked it little by little up and up until it met the other three walls. It didn't take long. There was a cheer from everyone when the walls met. More men went to work securing the new wall.

"This isn't all," said Pete. "There is another addition going up over on the east side of this that will house the stables and another addition on the west side that will house the bunks. This is a work building. If you are assigned here, you'll come for a few weeks or so and bunk with the rest of the men. You'll take your turn keeping watch, riding out to find cattle, tending sheep and maybe even do a bit of gardening."

A wagon train triangle bell rang out. A few men yelled, "Dinner!" The crews began cleaning up and packing tools away. Nate watched one man sweeping. "I should be doing that," he said.

"Don't steal another man's job," said Henry. "If you're needed, they'll let you know."

"We're losing the sun," said Sam.

"Yup," said Henry.

They said their good-byes and shook more hands as they walked to the horses. Nate didn't want to leave.

"How do I get a job out here," Nate asked Henry.

"First, you ask Ken. Then they'll tell you when it's time," said Henry. "I know it's hard to wait, especially when you're excited."

"Thanks, Henry," said Nate. A new feeling welled up inside Nate pushing out the old memory. Anticipation.

They made it back up the rocky hill to the orchards just as the light was slanting into gold. Henry coaxed his horse to a lope. Nate felt an electric shock go through Kane. Before he knew it, Kane was galloping.

He heard Henry yelling, "Just hang on! He knows the way home!"

It was scary, but Nate hung on as ordered. He thought, after this fantastic day, now he would die. Thoughts whizzed through his mind – Kane will misstep and go down crushing him – Kane will run so far that Nate won't know the way back in the dark – Kane will stop and throw him over into something hard and he'll break his arm or leg.

Nate saw the barn in the distance. Something dark inside him left. He leaned in, moved up and grabbed the saddle with his knees. He felt like a jockey and his heart was free. Kane responded with more speed.

A moment later Kane slowed to a lope on his own, then a canter, then a walk. Ten minutes later they were at the barn. Nate pulled up the reigns and Kane obediently stopped. He got off and began to lead him inside to his stall. He tried to control the shaking in his legs, but he was laughing. He knew he was going to be sore tomorrow.

"Hold up, there!" yelled Henry. "You'll need to walk him and wipe him down. Sam is saving his horse. You know this took a lot out of that old mare."

Nate followed Henry around the stables cooling the horses.

When Sam arrived, they went about the business of unsaddling and rubbing down their animals. When the horses were safely tucked into their stalls, fed, and watered, Nate was ravenous.

"Any sandwiches left?" he asked.

"Let's go see Cook," said Henry.

As they approached the front porch, they noticed a crowd forming on the front lawn.

Chapter 11

Nate and the others watched as the old man jumped out of his chair, flew off the porch and ran out beyond the group. Nate was amazed at how fast the old man could run, not awkward or limping or slow. He sprinted like a college athlete. Someone was coming over the crest of the hill illumined by the slanting orange light of sunset.

The old man met him as the person fell to the ground. The old man helped him up. They hugged. Cheers came from everywhere, the big house, the rest house, the yard, the woods, and the porch where Nate was standing. Nate found himself cheering too, though he wasn't sure why. The old man wrapped his strong arm around the new person and helped him walk back to the house.

As the group came closer Nate recognized Solomon, Caleb, Reuben, and Alex.

"I never get tired of watching that," said Cook, who was standing behind Nate. "Warms my heart."

"Who is that?" asked Nate, thinking it might be Miles, or maybe Joe.

"I shouldn't say, but you can meet him when he's rested. I'm preparing food for him. They'll take him to the Rest House first. They will want to be alone for a while. You go in now and get yourself something to eat."

Then Ken's voice boomed out from the lawn,

"Miles is back!"

"We're having a party tonight!" yelled Cook.

Everyone cheered.

Nate went to his room, strangely warmed in his heart, looking forward to the party. He found himself wishing he might see Joe again and that Alex would realize he was wrong about him.

Restless, he washed up and went back down to help.

Extra staff streamed into the kitchen from every door. The last light of day met the sounds and smells of grills, cakes and bread baking, potatoes boiling, vegetables simmering, and laughter. Excitement filled the house. Outside in the backyard tables were being set up. The wide southern doors to the dining room were opened to produce a huge dining area inside and out. Strung lights glistened. Someone built a bonfire. The last of the sunset seemed to extend itself.

Nate found an empty seat. Cook announced the kitchen staff would serve. A young girl Nate hadn't seen before came by and gave him a soda – his favorite. He thanked her. She seemed glum. "You're welcome," she said.

A distant memory dripped into Nate's mind, and he knew he had met her before.

People were walking past him saying, "Hi, Nate!" and "How are you, Nate?" and Nate was greeting them, no longer wondering how they knew his name, just knowing that everyone knew everyone, and he wanted to know everyone like everyone else.

Nate felt happy. Maybe he would be a Seeker someday, he thought. He knew he had a past, and he knew some of it was good and some of it was bad, but Henry and Sam had shown him what his future could be. He was excited about the day he could ride out to the New Building by himself and learn the ways of cattle and sheep. He was even looking forward to working in the garden.

Suddenly, Joe was sitting next to Nate at the table.

"Hi, Joe!" said Nate, happy to see him. "I've been looking for you. Where have you been?"

"You don't want to know," said Joe.

"Sure I want to know," said Nate, being as direct as his saddle mates had been with him. "But you don't have to tell me."

Joe looked sullen at that. Nate changed the subject. "Hey, have you been out to the orchards?"

"Sure," said Joe, "I been everywhere. What kind of fool do you think I am?"

Something turned inside Nate – something uneasy and sick. "Joe," said Nate quietly. "Alex told me you left out the back door."

Joe sneered. Nate's happiness vaporized.

They ate in silence while the other end of the table participated in a happy discussion of the talent of the cooks. Joe leaned over and whispered in Nate's ear, "Miles ran away last year. We haven't seen him since last summer. They say he went back to his drinking buddies in Arizona."

"But he came back," said Nate.

Joe shrugged.

Nate felt a chill on his shoulders, like he was sitting next to a block of ice. He looked over at Alex sitting at the next table and noticed he was looking at Joe. Nate nudged Joe in the ribs feeling like he was being pushed in the middle of something ugly. Joe pushed back – hard – glancing at Alex sideways as if he hated him. Nate wanted to move to another table but felt frozen in his seat.

The older lady sitting next to Nate on the other side asked him what his favorite food was.

"Hamburgers," said Nate, feeling foolish sitting next to Joe who was undoubtedly laughing inside. "But today I think my favorite is barbecued chicken and sweet corn."

"It is good, isn't it," said the lady.

Nate nodded, "Did Chef make it?" Nate was desperately trying to keep the conversation going so he wouldn't have to listen to Joe.

"Oh, I'm not sure. I think the sauce is the creation of Chef, but there are a lot of cooks and servers today."

At that moment, Cook appeared at the table.

"Hi, Cook," said Nate happily.

Cook replied by greeting everyone at the table by name and hoping they were having a good time. Everyone at the table was talking at once and Nate felt his tension ease. He glanced at Alex who was smiling as he talked to the man next to him. Then Nate turned to Joe and was surprised to find someone else was sitting where Joe had been.

Nate looked around but couldn't see where Joe had gone.

Chef was next to come over to the table. Everyone applauded. He took a seat across from Nate.

"Hi, Nate!"

"Hi, Chef!" said Nate, "Everything tastes wonderful."

"Well, I can only take credit for some of the sauces. Julie did the salads. Fred took care of the breads – he is a wonderful baker. Cook, potatoes – mashed, baked, herbed, sliced, cheesy, hash browns and twice baked. And we had so much help. Everyone chips in and everything gets done. This is a wonderful place to create meals."

Nate felt overwhelmed. It was strange for him to hear others praising others. A tiny memory irritated in the back of his brain. He closed his eyes and let it come. He was sitting in a darkened restaurant with some people he couldn't see clearly. He saw the fancy food at the table – lobster, cream sauce, asparagus, drinks, caviar – and he could almost smell it. From his left came a man who commanded respect. Perhaps he was the owner. He asked how the meal was and suddenly a woman to Nate's right began complaining about everything in a sultry, yet whiny voice. Nate was upset. He wanted to escape under the table, but he wasn't allowed. He was dressed up and sitting between a well-dressed gentleman and the unhappy extravagantly dressed woman. He could smell the strong perfume.

Nate kept his eyes closed and willed himself to look at the woman. He knew he shouldn't try to remember while celebrating at a party, but he had to know. She was dressed elegantly and had a beautiful sneer on her painted face. He knew in his heart this was not his mother. He tried to see the man sitting across from him, but Chef nudged him, and he came to himself.

"Sorry."

"I'm sorry, were you sleeping?" asked Chef.

"Not really." Nate studied Chef's face. "I was remembering."

"Oh," said Chef in subdued tones. "Care to share?"

Nate was happy that Chef wanted to know his memories. "I was in a restaurant. There was a lady complaining about the food, but the food was wonderful. I felt terrible. I wanted to slide under the table."

"Ah, yes," said Chef not smiling anymore. "The irritated, spoiled customer. I have had to deal with a few. You will never please them and they make everyone in the party uncomfortable. It doesn't matter how nicely you treat them. It doesn't matter how kindly you apologize, or ask the discussion to end, or try to move elsewhere. Somehow that just makes it worse."

"Yes." Nate was relieved Chef understood.

"Those people are never happy. It's as if they know the power they have over people and relish it, which makes them the most inconsiderate of all people. They have no respect for the feelings of others. The world is their playground. They believe they are making the world a better place by being in it, showing everyone how we are lacking and how perfect they are, when the opposite is true."

Nate nodded and was silent.

After a pause, Nate asked, "Do you know Miles?"

"Oh, yes," said Chef.

Nate decided to be direct. He was beginning to trust people and he knew that what Joe had told him might not be true because Joe was angry. "Did he really leave out the back door and go back to Arizona?"

Chef thought for a minute, choosing his words with care. "First, you must know, and you probably already know, that everyone here has a past. We are here because the old man saved us from our old lives."

"Yes, I know that. Henry said he doesn't like to remember. Sam said he remembers sometimes but doesn't think about it."

"That's right. I also had a dark past. Maybe you did too. I see you are remembering, and you are realizing the past is both good and bad."

Nate nodded.

"What we do with those memories is up to us. We can think about our past and wish we could go back to fix things or live that way again. We could go back to the people we think might still care about us. Or we can stay here and create a new life for ourselves. Or, as with Miles, we can do both."

"Oh, so he -"

"Yes, what Joe said is true. But why would he say it the way he did? Why would he make Miles out to be less than he is? Joe is angry and he will be leaving again soon, I have no doubt. He has said angry words to the old man and the old man has reminded him he could leave anytime. And he knows the old man will welcome him back."

"Yes, I know," Nate shook his head. "That makes me feel kind of good and weird and a tiny bit angry all at the same time."

Chef laughed. "That's a perfect way to put it!"

Nate smiled. He felt like the mystery of the ranch was beginning to open for him. He felt free. He was pretty sure he had not felt free in his old life.

"Miles was gone a long time. Here he was a leader and took on great responsibility. I have known him for as long as I have been here. We all love Miles and we knew he wanted to bring his family here. But it was not to be. Unless you really want to come, you will not come."

Nate suddenly had a flash of understanding. "So, I wanted to come."

"Oh, yes! I don't know about your old life, but if you didn't make the choice to come you would not be here now."

"But Joe said ..." Suddenly Nate was angry at Joe. Joe had lied to him again. He had twisted the truth to get Nate to leave.

Or maybe it was something else.

"It's okay, Nate," said Chef. "Try not to be angry with Joe. The best thing to do is ask the old man about your past. He will tell you what you need to know."

"I asked Alex and he said I would remember in time."

"Uh! Patience!" Chef laughed again. "I will have none of that!"

Nate laughed. "Thanks, Chef."

Chef put his hand on Nate's back. "I like talking to you, Nate. Maybe you want to help me in the kitchen one day."

"Yes," Nate announced. "That would be fun!"

"Oh, and another thing," Chef whispered in Nate's ear. "You probably don't want to hear this, but you need to read that book in your room."

Nate nodded.

"I'm sorry, I know it's hard, but it really helped me. I didn't read the book for almost a year."

"A year!" The guilt in Nate's chest dissipated.

"Yes, I am sorry to say, I am not a good example.

Have you read some?”

“Yes, I have. Three chapters.”

“That's wonderful! You are doing much better than I did! Now, if you will excuse me, I must help clean up.”

“I'll come too,” said Nate, picking up his dishes and following Chef.

In the kitchen Nate washed his dishes, then tried to stay out of the way. There were so many people helping. He spotted a full garbage bag and grabbed it, tied it and called, “Cook! Where does the garbage go?”

“Out that door and to the left!” Cook called back as she scrubbed a blackened pan.

Outside he found the large brown bins. He struggled to open one and threw the bag in. It slammed shut. He returned for something else to do.

He watched as silverware was dried and put away, dishes were stacked, and cups polished. Then he noticed the floor. There were spots and spills and smudges of unidentified things. He found a small sponge mop and went to work, dancing between helpers and he cleaned up spills. As the cleaners finished up one by one, he moved to do more floor cleaning. At last it was just Cook and Chef. He gave the dining room floor the once over, then inspected it. Perfect.

Nate felt satisfied. He looked at Cook and Chef and smiled. They smiled back. He was glad they didn't say anything. That would have ruined the moment.

He went out to the front porch and sat on a chair. There were always lots of chairs open and tonight there plenty of people enjoying them. He sighed and listened to the conversations and night noises.

“Getting late,” said the old man. There were people between them, but somehow Nate knew the old man was talking to him.

“Yes, Sir,” said Nate. “Just taking a little fresh air before going to bed.”

“Nate, may I speak with you,” said the old man.

"Sure." Nate moved across the porch to sit with the old man.

"Nate, you have been doing a wonderful job, pitching in, getting to know the staff and the other members of the family. Thank you."

Nate caught his breath and nodded. Something welled up inside of his heart. He didn't know what to say. He was afraid he was going to cry. After a moment he choked, "Someday I would like to work at the New Building, maybe learn how to run cattle and tend sheep ..."

"Someday you might," said the old man. "I don't want to dump cold water on your dreams, but there are others ahead of you, so to speak, others that have been here for years and want the same thing."

Nate felt the disappointment stab him, but he could understand.

"Nate, I hope you take this in the spirit in which it is intended. I would like to change your name, call you something a little different."

Nate stared at the old man. "Why?" he asked.

"Well, it's a little habit I have, I guess. Sam was called Samuel, but I shortened it because, well, he got the job done. He wasn't a sit-and-think kind of person. I felt Sam suited him better."

"I didn't know."

"Well, it was a special moment for him and me. You see, he didn't particularly like his name, for reasons he can tell you if he wishes, and when I suggested 'Sam' he was pleased."

"Yes, Sir, I see. It suits him."

"I think so. That leads me to you. When you first came here you were floating, not really knowing what you wanted, but in the few days you have been with us you have grown. You like helping people and you are eager to learn everything about this ranch. Not everyone wants to know everything that's going on. I can guarantee you that, if you continue as you have, and have patience, you will know everything about this ranch. Maybe even things you don't want to know.”

Nate was silent. He looked at his hands, wondering where this was leading.

“Nate, I would like your permission to call you Nathan.”

“Nathan?”

“Yes. You have grown as a person, and I think your name should grow with you.”

Nathan smiled. “Okay.”

“It's a little like when a woman gets married, she takes on the husband's last name. She grows, becomes more than what she was before. She has united two families. Do you understand?”

“I think so.”

The old man laughed a little, “I don't mean this is like getting married, but I do mean that you are growing, and your family is growing.”

Nate was feeling overwhelmed again. It was as if the old man loved him. How could that be? He barely knew him. Nate was afraid to speak. He didn't want to ruin it.

“Do you have questions about your past? I know, from what you told me, and from what I overheard you talking to others about – excuse my nosiness – you still haven't remembered much...”

“Well, I would like to know who that woman was.”

“Which woman is that?”

Nate explained the memory he had had at the celebration about the rude woman in the restaurant.

“Ah, yes, that woman. Well, I can't be sure, but it may have been your stepmother.”

Nate examined the old man's face hoping he would tell him more.

“Your parents were rich. Your mother disappeared many years ago, I think when you were eight or nine, and your father had her declared legally dead. Then he married another woman who didn't love him but loved his money. It was not a pleasant marriage. You were not happy."

"I know." The sick stomach was beginning to twinge.

"Would you like to know more?"

"Not right now, but thank you," said Nate. "I'm tired. I think I'll go to bed."

"Yes, of course." The old man stood and held out his hand. Nathan took it and shook it. The old man's hand was warm and strong. His arms were strong like he had worked hard every day of his life. His shoulders were broad and his whole body seemed to be younger than his face.

Nathan smiled and said good night.

As he moved away, a small child ran up the front steps and yelled, "Umpah!" He jumped into the old man's arms and squeezed him. The old man chuckled. The child was upset. Nathan watched a moment as the old man spoke soft and gentle words to the child he could not hear. Soon the child was talking too.

Nathan climbed into his bed and happily read two more chapters of the book. It was all beginning to make sense.

Chapter 12

Nathan awoke to yelling. He smelled smoke. Jumping out of bed he pulled on his jeans and, after feeling his door, rushed out to find the source of the noise.

He ran down to the first floor. The downstairs hallway was filled with people, so he ran out the front door and around to the east side of the house. Smoke was pouring from one window. A crew of seven men were taking turns with hoses and buckets.

On a hunch, Nathan ran back inside and up the stairs to the east hallway. Approximating which room was on fire, he ran to the door that would be above it and pounded. No answer. He pounded harder. Then he tried the knob. It was unlocked.

The room was filled with heat and smoke from below.

"Anyone in here!" he yelled. No answer. He held his breath against the smoke. He crossed to the window and opened it.

"Hose!" he yelled. A man on the ground threw one up to him.

Nathan poured water on the floor. Then he moved to the next room to see if anyone was still there. More people ran into the upstairs apartment. One of them was Miles.

"There she is!" said Miles pointing to another

room. "I got her!"

Miles carried out a young lady. Others sloshed through the wet carpet and located a child. At the sight of them the child began to cry. A woman caught him up in her arms and comforted him.

"Thanks," said a man.

"It's out!" someone yelled from outside. "Fire's out!"

"Is that everyone?" asked Nathan, checking all the rooms again.

"Yes, I think so," said another.

Nathan checked the ground before throwing the hose out of the window. He searched the soggy, smoky rooms one more time. Then he went outside to get some fresh air. His throat was sore. His head hurt. His eyes stung.

In the front yard some men were carrying Miles. Nathan grabbed Solomon's sleeve. "What happened?"

Solomon shook his head. "He wasn't supposed to be out of his room."

"What?"

Alex was beside Nathan. "Miles smelled the smoke and left his bed in the Rest House."

"Oh," said Nathan. "I hope he'll be okay."

"As long as he stays put," said Alex. "But you can't keep people from wanting to help."

Nathan glanced at Alex. "What happened?"

Alex met Nathan's eyes. Suddenly he knew, like a flash of light going off in his head as he made a mental calculation of doors.

"Joe."

Alex nodded.

Nathan felt a heavy weight on his chest. He was sad, disappointed, and angry. Joe must be crazy to set fire inside a place where people lived. As he walked back to his own room, he noted several men stationed at the four corners of the house, on the porch, at the stairs and in the hallway.

Security.

Nathan crawled back into bed exhausted and not bothering to take off his soaked clothes. But he couldn't sleep. He knew the men were well trained and ready, but somehow the Big House didn't feel safe anymore.

Chapter 13

Miles was up and about, talking to the nurses and joking with the janitors.

"Be careful on those legs, Miles."

"Yes, Sol."

"Do you need help getting back to your old room?"

"I don't think so," said Miles. "I'll yell if I do."

"No more running for a while," Solomon chuckled.

"Right."

"See you tomorrow."

"Yup."

Miles walked back to The Big House. "Welcome Home Miles" was tacked to his door. Inside his favorite snacks were on the table and the place smelled fresh. "Thanks," he said.

The old man had told him to rest for at least three days after being healed. As he was remembering this, he noticed the new three tier shelf full of books of all kinds. Miles smiled. "Looks like about 100 books," he said out loud. That should last him a day or two.

He chose "A Tree Grows In Brooklyn" and sat on the bed. Miles unstrapped the leg braces, doctor's orders. He covered himself with soft, warm, fragrant sheets. He thought of his family in Phoenix and felt sad. But he had done what he went to do. The rest was up to them. He remembered seeing Joe running away from the Big House after he smelled smoke. He was angry.

"Everyone has to make their own decisions," he said out loud, trying to calm himself.

His last thought as he got comfortable was "I'm home." He made it through two pages of his book and fell asleep.

Chapter 14

The dining room was packed so Nathan took a seat in the living room where lots of others were waiting for a seat as well. The evening was cool, and someone had started a fire in the fireplace.

"We do this every once in a while," said Alex to a young lady.

"The food smells good," she said.

Nathan tried not to eaves drop.

He desperately looked for someone to talk to. He smiled at the people sitting near him, they smiled back but were in conversation with someone else already.

"Nathan," said Alex, suddenly up close to him. "Come meet Staci."

Nathan nodded, suddenly feeling the same anxiety he had felt when Henry had put him up on Kane.

"Staci, this is Nathan," said Alex.

They exchanged greetings. Alex moved on to the next group to make conversation.

After a few minutes of awkwardness, Nathan asked, "So, how long have you been here?"

"This is my first day," said Staci looking at his shoes. Nathan got a flash of memory in his mind like an intense pinpoint of light. He had seen Staci two days ago serving at the celebration. She had given him a soda. This was not her first day. He decided to tread carefully. Maybe she couldn't remember. Maybe she was afraid.

"First day, huh. I remember my first day. Didn't know what to do with myself." Nathan ventured a glance at her. She had the tiniest of timid smiles on her face. "Did they give you a job yet?"

"Job?"

"You know, an assignment? Something to do?"

"No, I don't know ..." she trailed off.

Nathan waited. When no words were forthcoming, he plunged on. "Who's your Seeker?"

"Seeker?"

"Yeah, the person that brought you here."

"No one brought me here," said Staci. "I came here on my own."

"Really? How – how did you know about this place?"

"Oh, my mom told me. She used to work here. She always talked about it like it was the best place in the world to work. When I turned 18, I left and came here."

Staci was looking a little more comfortable. She grabbed the arms of her chair and pulled it closer to the fireplace. Nathan noticed she had no jacket. He also got the eerie feeling he knew her from someplace, maybe his old life. He wondered if she recognized him.

"Happy Birthday," said Nathan smiling and giving her his jacket. "It's a little worn but keep it as long as you need to."

"Thank you," she said, appearing embarrassed. "I left mine up in my room. And it's not my birthday."

"Oh, you just said when you turned 18 you came here ... and, um, this is your first day ..."

"My 18th birthday was last year. It's taken me this long to find the place."

"Wow. You really must have wanted to come here."

Staci shrugged her shoulders. Nathan was

wondering how she couldn't know where the ranch was when her mother had lived here. Things weren't adding up and that made him feel uncomfortable.

"Why isn't your mom still here? I mean, if she liked it so much, you know."

Nathan watched as something like pain grew in Staci's eyes. He felt bad but didn't like the feeling that he was being lied to. Maybe she wanted people to think she was someone else. Maybe he had asked the wrong questions. Maybe she would hate him. Maybe Alex would be mad about that. Maybe she couldn't remember and that made her embarrassed.

"I'm sorry," he said. "Um, do you want to go see if they have seats open yet? I mean if you don't mind eating with me. I mean if there's someone else you will be eating with."

"That's okay. Sure, let's go see." Staci moved quickly and Nathan had to hop a bit to keep up.

In the dining room a few seats were open. Someone came with drinks. The servers smiled. Staci and Nathan didn't have to ask for anything. The servers brought what each one of them liked.

They ate in silence. Nathan tried to think of something to say, but he was hungry. Then he tried to listen to the conversation around him but found it hard to concentrate. Then he looked for Henry and Sam. It seemed like he didn't know anyone in the room. He wished Staci would say something. He couldn't help thinking that he knew her from somewhere. The thought of someone from his bad past coming to the ranch was unsettling.

"Staci?"

"Hm?"

"May I show you around the ranch? Would you like a tour?"

"Sure," she said.

She is impossible to read, thought Nathan. I hope this isn't going to be painful.

After washing up their dishes, Nathan stopped in the kitchen. "Hi, Cook!"

"Hi, Nate!"

Nathan knew she was busy but led Staci over to meet Cook anyway. Somehow, he felt that this was important.

"Staci, this is Cook."

"Hi," said Staci quietly.

"Welcome, Staci. I'd heard you decided to join us. I'm kinda busy right now, but tomorrow morning you come talk to me before breakfast, ya' hear?"

"Yes'm," said Staci, smiling just a little. They waved to Cook and left the house by the front porch.

"You just tell me if you get tired," he said.

"Okay," she said.

He took her past the Rest House, then over to the stables to meet Henry, then to the schoolhouse, then the long walk out toward the gardens.

"I'm tired," she said.

"Well, maybe we can go on horseback another day," said Nathan. He noticed she seemed pale.

Staci nodded.

"Can I walk you back to your room?" he asked.

Fear sprung up in her eyes. Nathan was sorry he had made the suggestions. "Okay, no problem. I have to do my sweeping. I'll see you later." Nathan moved toward the Big House as Staci sat on the schoolhouse steps and looked around. He yelled out, "Nice meeting you!"

"Yeah," she said.

Nathan felt strange, like he had insulted her or done something wrong. He turned around. She was still sitting there looking around. Maybe she was just scared. Maybe she was disoriented like he had been. He didn't know what else to do. He entered the rear door of the Big House and started his work.

Chapter 15

The next morning there was a knock at Nathan's door. It was Joe. Nathan allowed him in but remained wary.

Joe was smiling.

"Hey, Joe, what's up? I thought you left."

"Just came to see how you're doing," said Joe looking around the room. "Love what you did to the place."

"Where have you been?"

"I went on a little trip," said Joe. His smile was crooked.

"Joe, what's wrong?"

"Well, Boy-oh, I woke up, you know what I mean? I know how this place works now. I'm leaving, and this time for good ... and I'm taking you with me."

"I don't want to go."

"Sure you do ... or have you gotten attached to the old man."

"Which old man are you talking about?"

"The front porch old man. The one we all take orders from."

"I think you should leave now," said Nathan, feeling a mix of fear and anger rising in his gut.

"You sound afraid, Boy-oh. What are you afraid of? Me? The old man? You're past? Huh? You know who you are? Have they told you yet? You know where you came from?”

“I don't think I came from New York like you said in your note.”

“Hah! Smart kid, aren't ya? Ah, well, you are right about that ... Nope. You are not from New York. A New Yorker would be smarter.”

Nathan had had enough. He pushed past Joe leaving his door open and walked down the hall to the stairs. He could hear Joe following him. He was headed to the front porch. He knew he could think clearly on the front porch.

As he reached the living room, he saw Sam sitting reading by the fire. Feeling relief he sat in a chair across from Sam waiting for Joe to come down the stairs.

“Hi, Sam. I need your help,” he said quietly.

“Sure, Nate, anything I can do,” said Sam leaning forward. Nathan noticed that Sam was tired.

“You look worn out today,” said Nathan

“Yes, just a little. That ride took it out of me I guess... and that party!”

“Do you need a healer?” asked Nathan, glancing at the stairs again.

“No, I don't think so. Just taking the day off.”

“Can I get you anything?”

“Oh, no. I'm fine, Nate. Just had a piece of Cook's apple pie. Have you tried that?”

“Yeah, it’s great.”

Sam stopped talking and looked at Nathan. “You look like someone who has a problem.”

“Joe's been bugging me.”

“Bugging you. Joe? I thought he was gone.”

“Me too, but he showed up in my room just now.”

“Well, you did the right thing. Sometimes people don't listen, and you need to find someone else to talk to them. Where is he?”

“He was behind me.”

Sam looked around. Then he struggled to get up. Nathan helped him. They walked to the foot of the stairs, but Joe was nowhere to be seen. Sam led Nathan out to the front porch where they found seats and got comfortable.

"Mornin'" said the old man.

"Morning, Sir," said Nathan.

"Good Morning, Sir," said Sam.

"Trouble?" asked the old man.

"Just a mite," said Sam.

The old man finished lighting his pipe. The sweet smell of tobacco wafted over to Nathan. He felt a calm come over him.

"Anything I can do?" asked the old man.

Sam was silent. He looked at Nathan.

"Joe was in my room," said Nathan. "I asked him to leave, but he wouldn't go."

"Ah," said the old man. "I guess starting that fire wasn't enough for him."

"I need some advice, Sir. What should I do?"

"You will have to confront him," said the old man. "Even though you may not want to."

"I did, but he didn't leave."

"You may not have been firm enough, confident enough. You need to stand your ground. He can't make you do anything you don't want to do."

Sam was nodding.

"I will give you this piece of advice," said the old man. "I don't like fighting on my ranch, but sometimes you must stand up for yourself with force. I'm guessing he's dangling information about your past in front of you, he was one of the Seekers that went to get you. He knows where you came from. Maybe it irritates you because he knows more than you do."

Nathan nodded.

"All that information about your past will come to you in time. Swallow your pride and let him tell you what he knows. If he doesn't then call him on it. He might just be bluffing. If it comes to blows, then, so be it."

A thrill of cold fear shot through Nathan's middle. He didn't want it to come to blows. The knot in his gut tightened. He knew there might be a fight because Joe was so angry.

"Okay," Nathan said.

After some thinking, Sam said, "Nathan, I think I'll sit out here for a bit."

"Okay."

"You got work to do?"

"Oh, yeah. I'll see ya. Thank you for the advice, Sir."

"You are welcome. Come talk to me any time."

Nathan was irritated because he knew the old man was right. He always wanted to run from confrontation, but he didn't know why.

It didn't take him long to get the first floor swept. It was good therapy. It didn't take him long to get the upstairs vacuumed. That was good therapy too.

Then he saw it - another set of stairs, leading to a third floor.

He decided to explore.

The stairs were steeper which got him thinking that it might be an attic. As he climbed the creaky stairs, he heard music. It sounded like old music, scratchy and dusty. A dim light was coming from somewhere.

As he emerged, he saw the huge open space was filled with storage.

One corner looked as if someone had used it as a bedroom a long time ago. Lava lamps, psychedelic wallpaper, and an old hi-fi stereo were arranged around an old wood-framed single bed. Nathan walked over slowly, humming a little just in case someone else was up there too. He didn't want to startle them. He remembered a stereo just like that one in his aunt's house. The lid was up, and the vinyl record was moving around and around. The music was crackly, and he didn't recognize the song, but it was slow and sad. The unmade bed was a mass of dingy blankets and pillows. On the walls were pictures of people he didn't recognize, politicians and musicians and actors.

The music was creeping him out, so he switched it off.

"Hello?" he called out. He strained to hear something; his voice sucked up into the soft silent atmosphere.

It was a little stuffy, so he went looking for windows to open. This floor will have to be swept and dusted, he thought. He passed several places that looked like bedrooms divided by stacked boxes of all sizes, furniture, and foldable room dividers. There seemed to be a layer of dust over everything. In each area were strange things, some he recognized from his past: a doll house that had a small sign on it that said it was magical, a contraption that looked like it was used in weather forecasting, and lots of stuffed animals.

A path flowed from one temporary room to the next. It wound back and forth through the attic. Nathan stopped partway. To the right was a window, brown and dingy. He wiped off some of the dust and cobwebs. Then he tried to open it. After a bit of effort he noticed that it had been painted shut. He would have to come back with tools.

Maybe he would have to get permission. Maybe this was a place of memories that people went to feel better. Maybe he wasn't supposed to touch anything.

He made his way to the other end of the room. Here was a window that he could open. The breeze was sweet and swept past him like fresh air clearing out a tomb. He looked out at the beautiful view. The window seemed to be directly over the front porch, and he could see further over the grassy hill. He could see the fields, hills, and mountains beyond. It was beautiful. He wanted to stay. This is better than my room, he thought.

Nathan found a random chair in the boxed-in-room nearest the window and pulled it over to sit. The breeze swayed the monstrous trees near the house making a sound like waves on the ocean. It felt like the weather was changing. He took a deep breath. Rain.

As Nathan sat in the attic, he felt like he was someplace else. Suddenly, he recognized all his things from his old room at his old house. He smiled. There was his bed, the quilt his grandmother had made for him, his clothes hanging on a makeshift one-inch pipe rack against the wall, the boxes piled high to the ceiling. His sketches, long forgotten, were pinned on the box-walls. There was the sketch of his mother – the one his father had thrown away.

And then he remembered. Like the whoosh of the wind when opening the window, Nathan became his old self.

And he knew his name wasn't Nathan. He knew The Ranch was not his home. He knew these were his precious things from his past. This small space felt like home, comfortable, drowsy. He remembered good times, trips to the library, days at the beach, Saturday morning cartoons, camping trips, days in his room with nothing to do but draw.

Nathan enjoyed the silence for a long time. Maybe he would spend the night in his old bed.

"Hey, Nate, how's it going? Or should I call you Nathan. Yeah. Nathan, because you earned it." Joe was speaking through his teeth as if he were gripping a cigarette.

"Hi, Joe," said Nathan, his stomach tightened. The words of the old man echoed in his head. It was time.

Nathan stood and faced Joe. "What are you doing up here?"

"I live up here, Nate. Who do you suppose started the stereo?"

"Like the fire?"

Joe laughed.

The pleasant remembering had ended. Now he was waiting. He planned to choose his words as carefully as he could. He wanted to stay here, but not if Joe remained to torment him.

"I supposed you're wondering why I'm up here," Joe said. "Well, you found it. This is your past. Congratulations! Now you know where you're from. Now you know who you are."

"Not really."

"Sure you do, Nate. Just look." Joe found a picture. "Here's you with your mom and dad. Remember?" He found a newspaper. "And here's your mom's obituary. Want to read it again? Or do you have it memorized?"

Nathan couldn't remember his mom much. The dart Joe threw had missed the mark.

"Joe, this is getting old. Let's go get some coffee," said Nathan, holding in his anger.

Joe laughed. Nathan closed the window. It was time to leave.

The sun was setting. A sudden realization that he had been up in the attic all day hit him like a big mistake. With a new resolve Nathan walked past Joe along the path back to the stairs.

"Hey! We're not done yet!" yelled Joe.

"That's fine," said Nathan, keeping his voice calm. "I'm going down to the kitchen to get some coffee. Want to join me?"

Suddenly there was a rush as Joe slammed Nathan with a tackle. Nathan pulled himself up and pushed Joe off.

"Leave me alone!" said Nathan. "What's ... I never did anything to you."

Nathan started walking away again trying not to limp. This time he heard the rush and stepped aside. Joe went crashing into a couch. Boxes went flying. Nathan tried to stay calm as his adrenalin kicked in. Joe threw a box and it hit Nathan in the back, pitching him forward. Nathan staggered a bit. He was almost to the stairs.

Joe was picking up a large metal sculpture of a sea gull. Nathan grabbed the old record off the stereo and held it in front of him like a shield. Joe stopped. His chest was heaving, and his face was red.

"Is this your memory, your past?" asked Nathan gesturing to the room he was standing in. "Did you grow up in the 1970s? Or is this your dad's stuff?"

"What do you care? You don't even know who your real dad is!" yelled Joe.

"My real dad?" asked Nathan, struggling to keep his voice steady.

"Yeah ..."

"You're going to tell me who my read dad is?"

"Sure."

"Well, then tell me. I'm done playing this game, Joe." Nathan placed the record back and started down the stairs. He kept to the wall, clutching the railing, just in case Joe decided to come at him with something else.

"I'll tell you! I'll tell you!" Joe yelled. Nathan paused. He looked up at Joe.

There was silence. Maybe Joe didn't know. Nathan had a sudden sick feeling that maybe Joe had a screw lose somewhere.

"He's the richest man in the world, that's who."

"And who would that be?" asked Nathan. "You're just making this up."

"His name is ..."

Nathan was watching Joe. Joe was struggling with something, his face growing still redder. Suddenly Nathan understood.

"You aren't supposed to tell me, are you? Someone told you not to tell me."

Something broke inside Joe. He exploded, "Phil Amor! That's your dad. Phil Amor! The nastiest bastard that ever lived. That's your dad. There! Now deal with it. I bet you'll be leaving. No more the favorite of the old man. Why should you stay? You stand to inherit all that dirty money. Your evil daddy can get you anything you want."

Nathan walked up the steps to be closer to Joe. "No, Joe. He can't. This Phil Amor person doesn't love me, otherwise why would I be here? The old man loves me. I know who I am."

As Nathan walked down the narrow stairs, he was mulling this news over. The name of Phil Amor jostled in his mind. Maybe he hadn't remembered everything.

Joe yelled down at him, "... and Staci is your little brat sister!"

Nathan paused, then continued to walk deliberately as he chewed on those final words. Somehow, he knew Joe was right.

He sat down in a living room chair. Joe didn't follow him. As the adrenaline wore off, Nathan felt overwhelmed and exhausted. He relaxed and let the memories come. His fear of failure because of the beatings he endured at the hand of his father, his sorrow over his mother's disappearance, no funeral to let him mourn. He couldn't stop the tears.

He wiped his face. It was dark and there was a small fire in the fireplace. Suddenly, all he wanted to do was sleep.

Nathan went back to his room. On the nightstand was water and aspirin with a note telling him to take it right away. He did and promptly fell asleep.

Chapter 16

Staci wanted to talk to Cook, but she couldn't find her in the kitchen.

"Where's Cook?" she asked the lady at the sink.

"Don't know, Staci. This is her day off," said the lady at the sink. "You might try The Rest House. She goes there sometimes."

Staci jumped down the stairs on the front porch. Several people greeted her, but she ignored them.

Staci opened the glass door to the Rest House.

"Good morning, Staci. Can I help you?" said Jane.

Staci frowned. They had never been introduced but Jane knew her name.

"I came to see Cook."

"Okay," said Jane. She made a call and had a short discussion in a language Staci did not understand. As she hung up, she said, "Someone will be right down to talk to you."

Staci paced. Then she sat in one of the seats.

An older lady appeared in the room. "Staci?" she said.

"Yes," said Staci.

"My name is Amethyst," said the lady. "Would you come with me, please?"

"Where is Cook? I want to talk to Cook," said Staci.

Staci followed the lady past the window

overlooking the pool and a few interesting doors.

"You don't mind stairs, do you?"

"No," said Staci. "Are we going to see Cook?"

Amethyst replied, "Just a moment, please."

They climbed the next set of stairs to the third floor which opened into a huge room filled with dappled amber light and calming music and couches and chairs and tables and what looked like beds and rice paper room dividers. The lady led her to a short hallway leading to a door that opened into a restaurant-like room full of people sitting around tables talking.

"Cook is with her Listener at the moment, but you are welcome to wait here. Please let me introduce to you a few of our Listeners. This is Maria," she continued motioning, "And Ruby and Jade."

"Hi," said Staci.

"I know this might be frightening, but we do things a little differently here. We sit and talk until you choose someone who you feel comfortable with."

"I just came to see Cook," said Staci, her voice barely audible. She felt overwhelmed and afraid. For the next 10 minutes she sat looking at the floor, listening to the conversation around her, wishing she had her cell phone. Why did they have to take her phone away?

One of the ladies stood up and walked over to Staci. "Hi, I'm Ruby. Would you like to talk?" Her voice was soothing.

Staci said nothing. "It's okay. We can just talk here or go out in the big room. If you and I aren't hitting it off, we can choose another person who would be a better fit."

"It's okay," said Staci, shrugging her shoulders.

"Let's find a place to sit..."

Staci nodded and followed Ruby out the door, down the hall and to a drink station, where Ruby poured herself a cup of coffee. "What would you like?" she asked.

"I like green tea," said Staci. Ruby showed her the

vast selection of teas and Staci chose one, made her tea and followed Ruby to a couch and chair. Ruby took the couch after Staci chose the chair.

"I am going to take you through some memory exercises," said Ruby.

"But when do I get to see Cook?"

"I'm sorry you can't talk to Cook right away, but you will see her soon. I don't know how long she will be. You will have to be patient, okay?"

"Okay," said Staci pressing her lips together and staring at her teacup. The cup had a red and orange dragon wrapped around it with the tail flowing up the handle. Staci memorized the detail.

"I hope you will talk with me a little today. This is what Cook and her listener are doing right now."

Staci relaxed.

"Maybe you could share a memory? It is not good that your memories are not coming back. You are holding things inside which are preventing you from enjoying your life here at The Ranch."

Staci nodded. They began. The talking was uncomfortable, but Ruby assured her that she would not share any information with anyone.

Staci shared some things that she never thought she would ever tell anyone. Memories came back. It was unpleasant. She held back the urge to cry.

Staci finally said she was tired and that seemed to satisfy the Listener.

When Staci walked back to her room in The Big House, she knew she never wanted to see Ruby again.

Chapter 17

Staci sat in her room and cried huge balls of regret. She had shared way too much. All she had wanted to do was talk to Cook. Cook never pried information out of people.

But she didn't have a choice.

Once again someone had said they would spend time with her, treat her right, be concerned about her, care about her, and maybe even love her, and once again, they did not. She felt as if she would explode or break apart. She wished she could melt away to a peaceful place where she was safe, warm, well-fed, and well-dressed. Or maybe just melt away into the ground and be gone.

Staci didn't want much. She just didn't want to be in pain anymore. She was tired of pain and thought somehow there was something cursed about her because everyone else around her was happy. How could it be that they were happy, and she was in pain? It didn't make sense.

Maybe they were in pain too and had learned how to hide it, maybe even convincing themselves that they were no longer in pain, or maybe they had finally found a place to belong, a place where people accepted them so they could be content and not worry about sudden attacks of bitter, poisonous words or hits and screams or people trying to use your personal information to own you.

There was a knock at her door. "Just a minute," she called in a squeaky voice. She wiped her face and went to the door.

It was Alex. Staci didn't like Alex.

"Hi, Alex," Staci said not really looking at him.

"Hi, Staci, I came to check on you. Was that the wrong thing to do?" Staci could hear the "caring" in his voice and it irked her.

"It's okay." She left the door open and went back to sit in her chair. Her room was too small, only a bed, a trunk for clothes and things, a chair, and a tiny end table with some dusty old book she was supposed to read. Her tiny bathroom was irritating to use. She couldn't even get the bedroom window open.

"I came to get you for lunch, if that's okay," Alex said.

Staci shrugged. "I'm not really hungry."

"Oh," said Alex. Then he just stood there looking around her room. This pushed her irking to anger. He was really getting on her nerves. "Well, Staci, you have to eat."

She hated the way her name sounded when he said it. She knew he was going to stand there until she said she'd come down, so she did. "I'll be down in a bit. I need to clean up first."

"Okay," said Alex smiling, "I'll save you a spot."

She got up and opened her trunk as if she were getting her things. After he left, she walked over and slammed the door. But it didn't make that sharp satisfying retort she had expected. It was muffled, as if the door was a pillow. Now she felt crushed.

In her bathroom, the smallest of bathrooms, she washed her face, brushed and put back her hair. She would wear her jeans and sweatshirt because that was the only thing she had – the clothes she came with. She wiped down the sink and shut out the light. The lady next door had said she was fortunate to have her own bathroom, but somehow it didn't help the fact that it was so small.

Down in the kitchen she tried to walk past Cook, angry that she hadn't been there when she needed her. But as usual, Cook had eyes in the back of her head.

"What did I tell you?" Cook asked.

Staci walked over to her and, on tiptoe, gave her a peck on the cheek as Cook leaned over to receive it.

"Kiss the cook," whispered Staci.

Cook chuckled and continued peeling potatoes.

"Thank you, Honey. What'll ya' have today?" Cook asked.

"I'm supposed to meet Alex out in the dining room," said Staci.

"And what's wrong with Alex?" Cook asked looking Staci in the eyes this time.

"Nothing, I guess."

"Sit."

Staci found a high stepstool chair and sat next to Cook.

"I'm sorry we didn't get to talk at the Rest House, Staci," said Cook.

"That's okay," Staci said in a whisper.

"I know you got a problem with men," said Cook in a sort of scolding voice (that Staci knew meant "I love you.")

"I did too when I got here. But you are just going to have to figure out how you are going to get over that. Alex is THE nicest man at this ranch. If he's taking special care of you, it's because the old man has a job for you – an assignment. Alex is here to help you get ready."

"I can't do anything. I don't see why they brought me here to begin with."

"That's what I thought too. Then this old lady comes up to me, slaps me in the back of the head and says to me, 'shape up and peel these potatoes.' Then I said, 'I don't know how.' Then she said, 'Watch.' I did and then she handed me a knife and told me to do the whole pile. Looking back, I think she must have been shaking her head. I cut off more potato than peel, but she said nothing. She just washed dishes and cut meat until I was done. Then she told me I did a good job."

"But you didn't. She was lying."

"No. That lady never lied in her life. She said I did a good job because I did it. I stuck with it until it was done. That's doing a good job."

Staci pondered.

"Don't matter if it's good or bad – just get it done."

"Okay. Can I go eat now?"

"Yes, you can. And you don't have to sit next to Alex if you don't want. You can just eat in here if you like."

"Thanks, Cook," Staci said as her face brightened just a bit and she smiled. Staci grabbed a sandwich and some chips. She sat and ate as she watched Cook. "You're fast."

"Should be. Been here long enough."

"Is that all you do? I mean, just cook and clean?"

"Isn't that enough?"

"Well -"

"I know what you mean," Cook said as she placed the peals in a large bucket and popped the potatoes in two large pots of water. "I tried a couple of things but cooking and kitchen work just made me feel good. So I stuck with it."

"And that was okay with the, um, the owner of the ranch?"

"As long as we are doing our job it's fine by him. You can call him the old man. Just about everyone does. Some calls him Ken. Some calls him Dad. There was a really old man that used to call him Father."

"Father ... sounds weird."

"Yeah, I thought so too, but he was an old-timey kinda guy, you know? From way back when this ranch was first built."

"How long have you been here?"

"Oh, a long, long time. Since I was about your age. I don't count the years."

"I can't remember what my last name is."

"Oh, that's okay. No one uses last names around here anyway. If you're supposed to remember, you will. Might take some time. Maybe you won't ever remember, and that's okay too."

"But I want to remember. I know I have family somewhere. I know they are missing me. I know they want me to come back."

Cook said nothing. Cook had an idea where Staci had come from. It was about the same sad, brutal life that she had had. There was no going back because going back meant death ... or worse.

"What's your real name? Cook is just what you do."

"Well, Cook isn't just what I do, it's what I am. Some here call me Pearl. It's an okay name. I got it the day I arrived, like you. I don't think about my old name anymore. My old life is gone, gone, gone. I am so so happy I ain't never going back."

For a moment Staci thought Cook was going to start singing. She placed her dishes on the sink and started for the door to the living room.

"Hold up there, Honey. You need to wash them dishes."

Staci hung her head as she walked back. She washed the dishes and dried them and placed them on the pass-through counter. She paused for a moment, watching. Then asked, "Can I help?"

"Sure 'nuff!" announced Cook. She chuckled a little and handed her a knife.

Staci cut off more potato than peel, but she got the job done.

Chapter 18

The next morning Nathan awoke to a knock at the door. As he called, "Just a minute," he noticed a room divider was placed near his bed hiding the door.

"Hi," Nathan said.

A well-dressed man stood in the doorway.

"Hello. Are you Nathan?"

"Yes, can I help you?"

"The Old Gentleman sent me to find you. He thought you might be interested in going on a short trip with me."

"A trip. Off the ranch?"

"Yes, that would be it. May I come in? I should explain it to you before you decide if you want to go or not."

Nathan invited the man in and noticed another chair had appeared next to his reading chair. Nathan felt a little embarrassed. "I'm sorry," he said, gesturing around the room. "I usually don't have guests."

"That's quite alright. You were not expecting me. May I introduce myself? My name is Edward Thomas, and I am a Seeker."

"Oh," said Nathan, pulling a hand through his mussed hair.

"The Old Gentleman wants you to see what we do. Do you have plans for today?"

Nathan thought for a moment. "No, I don't think

so."

"Good. If you don't mind, could you get ready for a day trip? I will meet you near the living room fireplace in, say, an hour. Is that enough time?"

"Yes."

Edward Thomas shook hands with Nathan and left, closing the door silently behind him. He reminded Nathan of a well-mannered butler from a mystery novel.

As they left the old man was on the porch talking with some people Nathan did not know. He pulled himself away from the intense discussion long enough to wave a greeting to Nathan and Edward Thomas as they walked down the porch steps. Nathan paused for a moment to listen to the language he had never heard.

"This way," called Edward Thomas, who had walked to the left as Nathan had gone to the right to get to the stables. "We will be taking a car. We are going into town."

"Oh," said Nathan with a little laugh. Embarrassed, he looked around to see if anyone has seen his mistake.

The car seemed old. It was silver gray, the kind of car that wouldn't bring attention to itself. Nathan had a memory of a game he had played naming make and model of the cars they passed. He remembered the game being highly competitive but couldn't remember who he played it with. The game seemed pointless to him now.

They drove for a long time. Nathan watched out the passenger side window trying to recognize the landscape. He was in a place he didn't think he had ever been before and something like sickness began to build inside of him. He was away from the safety of the ranch and with someone he didn't know going to an unknown destination. He felt completely helpless and out of control. He tried to take comfort in the fact that the old man had waved to him, so Edward Thomas must be okay.

"We are in enemy territory now," said Edward

Thomas, pulling Nathan out of his reverie.

"What do you mean?" A sudden wave of fear flowed through him as he recognized fences, trees, and outbuildings.

"This is Amor Lands. Phil Amor would probably not want us here, but this highway is public and the town to which we are going is also public."

Nathan's thoughts turned to his cruel father and what might happen if they were caught on his property.

"I'm sure I cannot explain it the way The Old Gentleman could," said Edward Thomas. "I will never be as clear as he. However, by now you know that Phil Amor is our employer's sworn enemy. His property abuts ours. He has created trouble for The Old Gentleman on and off for many years and it is no secret that he wishes to acquire our ranch for his own."

Nathan nodded suddenly wishing he was back in his room, reading that old book.

"We are driving through his property, and we must conduct ourselves as properly as possible. His hired thugs are everywhere and would love to engage us in a confrontation. We will avoid that at all cost. We will, most likely, meet some of his employees while we are in town."

When they arrived, Edward Thomas stopped the car in front of an old diner. The Main Street was dusty, and the buildings were two storied from the era of shop downstairs, living quarters upstairs. The windows of the diner were smudged with dried mud spatter from the last rain and passing cars.

Nathan followed Edward Thomas through the squeaking door and a bell above him rang. The smell of frying hamburgers, French fries and coffee sent a wave of nostalgia through Nathan's body. They found a seat near the rear of the building.

Nathan listened to conversations as his companion quietly ordered for the both of them. The waitress had to lean down to hear.

"Keep your voice low," said Edward Thomas. "We are here to observe only."

Nathan nodded and saw Reuben enter the diner.

"Is that a Seeker from the ranch?" Nathan whispered.

Edward Thomas nodded. He whispered back, "If we remain quiet, we can see how he works."

Then he added, "This is Reuben's first time alone."

Reuben chose a seat at the bar and ordered coffee. Nathan thought his voice seemed too loud. Reuben leaned over to the young man next to him and said, "Do you know Alex?"

The young man gave him a look of irritation. "Nope. Never heard of him."

"He's a great guy to know," said Reuben. "He saved my life."

"Really," said the man to his plate of ketchup covered French fries, inching away from Reuben.

"Yeah, want to meet him?"

"Why?" Now the young man was gesturing to the waitress with his head.

"He can save your life, too."

"My life don't need savin'."

"Reuben, this is not the way," Edward Thomas whispered to himself.

"Everybody's life needs saving." said Reuben.

"Really."

"Don't you have troubles?"

"Everybody has troubles."

The young man's shoulders pulled back, and he faced Reuben. "You're going to have trouble if you don't leave me alone."

Reuben rushed on, "Won't you tell me yours?"

Nathan closed his eyes waiting for the right hook. Edward Thomas held his breath.

Suddenly, Alex appeared, placing himself between Reuben and the young man. He was whispering in Reuben's ear, but somehow Nathan could hear. "This is not the way, Reuben. Can't you see he's not ready for this conversation?"

"I've got this. I know what I'm doing," argued Reuben.

"Gracefully excuse yourself."

The three words landed on Reuben with such force that he flinched.

"Sir," said Reuben to the young man, "I'm sorry I interrupted your meal. Please excuse me."

The young man shrugged his shoulders. Reuben left the diner. Alex paid for his coffee as well as the young man's meal. He wished him a good day. The young man watched Alex as he followed Reuben.

At the table Nathan felt embarrassed. Edward Thomas thanked the waitress for the burgers that had just arrived. The two ate in silence.

Back outside, Alex called to Reuben. He motioned discreetly toward a homeless man sitting on the steps of the vacant store front near the diner.

"Please wait for me to tell you who to talk to about coming to work for us," said Alex.

"He looked like someone we could use," said Reuben.

"The old man chooses who works for us. He has done so much research on each prospective employee. It's not possible for anyone else to know who will fit at the ranch. I don't expect you to understand. You just have to trust the old man."

Reuben nodded.

"This young man was not ready," said Alex. "He might have been ready by next year, but now we will have to wait and see. After pressing him, he may never be ready."

Those words hung in the air for a few minutes.

"I will tell you which person you should offer a job to," said Alex.

"Okay," said Reuben.

"The right person is sitting there waiting for you,"

said Alex.

There were tears in Reuben's eyes.

"Would you like to try again?"

"Yes," said Reuben.

Alex handed Reuben a brown sack lunch.

Reuben approached the man who looked up at him with disdain.

He handed the man the bag lunch saying nothing. The man's attention switched to the bag. He grabbed it, inspected the sandwiches, and devoured its contents.

"Do you think you might need more?" asked Reuben.

The man nodded.

"I know where you can get three squares a day," said Reuben.

The man stiffened. Reuben waited a bit, just sitting next to the man, fighting to be patient. He remembered the words Alex had told him. "This is your job, and maybe your calling. Take your time. Don't rush it. Be patient. You have all day, all weekend, all week. Just spend time with him. Some take longer than others. Some come right away. Some never come."

Alex was suddenly at his right arm handing him another bag. Reuben looked up to say thank you, but Alex had disappeared again. This unnerved him, but he knew he'd have to get used to it. Reuben also knew it was part of his control issues, the ones he talked about with Amethyst.

He handed the man another bag.

The man grunted. "Where'd you get the food?"

"From my friend, Alex," said Reuben.

"Got all the food in the world, huh?" the man seemed angry and bitter. "Has so much he's giving it away."

"Yes," said Reuben.

"You want something?" asked the man.

Reuben waited before speaking. He knew this man could twist whatever words he gave to suit his mood. He didn't want to make the same mistake he had made in the past – rushing people, pushing people. He stared at the street in front of him as the man ate. From the aroma these were Cooks special roast beef on rye.

"There's always a catch," said the man between bites. "What's the catch this time?"

Reuben waited, not knowing what to say. The man carefully folded the sandwich wrappings and the paper bag. He leaned up against the building and sighed, his eyes closed.

"Now I suppose you want me to go with you."

"If you like. It's up to you."

"So you'd just walk away if I said, 'No.'"

"Yes."

"Okay," said the man defiantly, speaking to the street, "I say, 'No.'"

Reuben got up and heard Alex whisper in his ear, "His name is Mack."

"Nice to meet you, Mack." said Reuben offering his hand which the man refused.

Reuben was suddenly hit with a gut full of compassion. He saw the Navy tattoo hidden under his sleeve. He saw the proud service of 10 years in his eyes. He noted the dog tags hidden beneath three t-shirts.

Reuben remembered his Army training, snapped to attention, and saluted the man. "Thank you for your service, Sir. Will there be anything else, Sir?"

"At Ease, Soldier," said Mack. Reuben saw tears forming in his eyes. He went to At Ease. After a moment he took a seat next to him. Inside he felt a welling up of loyalty and he knew he would be sitting next to this man for as long as he was needed.

Back in the diner Nathan was crying. He didn't know how he had seen the event outside, but it didn't matter anymore.

Edward Thomas was saying, "Thank you, Alex," under his breath.

With a sharp intake of breath Nathan suddenly

remembered. "This is the diner!" he croaked.

Edward Thomas seemed to sense Nathan's memory coming back and placed his hand on his shoulder. "Let it come. We'll stay as long as you need."

Flashes in scenes became a linear memoir in Nathan's mind.

Nathan had been sitting at the same seat by the bar as the young man. Joe had come in and had sat next to him in much the same way as Reuben offering to buy him lunch. Nathan could remember the fear that had filled his mind and his heart.

"Just leave me alone," Nathan said.

"Dude, I was just joking about paying for your meal. Just introducing myself."

"What do you want?"

"I got a job for you," said Joe.

"I already got a job, I don't want another one," said Nathan.

"Mine pays better. You get free room and board. You won't have to live in this dump anymore."

"What?"

"I saw your place. Real dump. The guys that come to see you aren't real nice either."

Nathan had been terrified. This guy knew too much about him. "You gonna arrest me?"

Joe laughed. "No. It's not like that. I'm just in from out of town and looking for employees for my boss."

Nathan felt a tiny spark of hope. "What's the work?"

Joe seemed apologetic as he said, "Boring stuff mostly. Gardening, cleaning, cooking, maybe working with horses ... stuff like that."

At the word "horses" Nathan heart flickered with hope. But something inside snapped. Joe was so confident, and Nathan felt the awful too-good-to-be-true feeling coming back. His life had always been a mess. Why would this guy want to hire him?

Nathan pushed Joe away and said, "Leave me alone."

"Hey," said Joe pushing back, "Just doing my job."

Their fight was quick and awkward. Nathan remembered seeing Alex come up to stop it. He remembered a left to his temple and all going black. The memory brought back the pain.

He had awakened in his tiny room above the bar. Alex was there placing ice on his head. Joe was sitting in a chair sulking against the wall. Nathan was waiting for the next attack, but none came. He fell asleep. The next thing he remembered was waking up in his room at the ranch and wondering where he was.

Edward Thomas studied Nathan as he wiped his eyes.

"How do you feel?" he asked.

"Okay," said Nathan. "I don't feel sick like the last time."

"That's good," said Edward Thomas. "We can go back now if you like. I believe the purpose of this trip is served."

Suddenly, Nathan felt queasy, and he shut his eyes. He heard Edward Thomas say, "Ah. Another."

Nathan nodded. Edward Thomas paid the diner bill and took Nathan back to the car.

On the trip back to the ranch Nathan lay on the bench seat in the back and remembered the awful things that were done to him and the ugly things he had to do.

He remembered being beaten by his dad, the one they called the enemy, Phil Amor.

He remembered even worse from men who threw money at his dad as they left.

He groaned.

"We'll be home soon," said Edward Thomas.

"Home," said Nathan. "Home. Hey, Ed, tell the old man I never want to leave the ranch again."

“You got it.”

Chapter 19

That night, after all the Big House was quiet, Staci enacted her plan.

Cook had been nice, and she enjoyed working with her, but there was something else that she needed. Nobody understood that.

She found the small storeroom off the kitchen, the one she had peeked into while someone was cleaning it the day before. This was the first aid room and had special pills that made her feel better. The ones she really needed after her talk with The Listeners, who she secretly called "The Priers."

She let herself in, locked the door behind her and climbed the cabinet.

The highest cabinet door latch was stuck tight. Staci climbed down from the counter and dug through drawers. Ahah! A screwdriver.

At home, "her past" as they all liked to call it, Staci was called "the monkey" because she could climb up anything and open anything. She frequently got in trouble for it, but she didn't care, she was short. She had to survive. They were all just jealous.

She climbed back up on the counter space to reach the latch. She had to get it open. She could see inside the pills she needed desperately. She wedged the metal bar of the screwdriver between the door and the latch and used all her strength to move it toward her. It budged.

A new wave of hope filled her with fresh energy. She yanked at it as it moved just a little more. Shaking it broke the latch. She paused to listen. Then she took a deep breath and opened it.

She read a few labels and found the ones she needed. As she grabbed the pills, she heard Cook's voice in her head, "Honey, you don't need those." She shook it off.

Take the pills, rearrange the bottles to hide the missing one, clean up the mess, out the door, she thought. Into her shirt they went.

As she landed on the floor, the door she thought she had carefully locked squeaked behind her.

"No, Staci," said Alex gently. "This is not the way. Come with me. We will go through this together."

Staci wanted to run, but there was no place to go. She handed the bottle to Alex who took her hand and led her out of the room. She felt relieved that no one was around to watch. They walked across the lawn to the Rest House.

Alex did not stop at the unmanned reception desk but walked straight through the first floor to a door.

Inside Alex motioned to the tall doctor and said, "Staci, this is Solomon. You will be staying here for a while, for as long as it takes. You will not leave. You will do everything Solomon tells you until you are free."

Staci nodded her head. This felt worse than the first time she was arrested. She could feel the bugs moving in her blood stream. Her head was getting worse. Her body ached.

Another lady walked in. "I'm Amber," said the lady. "I will be your Listener for your stay here."

Staci shrugged. Amber smiled and added, "I promise not to pry. You don't have to tell me anything you don't want to. Okay?"

Staci nodded. She looked at Amber. Something in her face helped Staci believe it would be okay. They were about the same age. Maybe this time would be different. Maybe this time she was tired enough of running and hiding and being in pain.

Amber showed her to her special room. They talked for a time about nothing important. Then they did some reading. Amber liked the same books as Staci. Amber even gave Staci new ones by Staci's favorite authors.

Feeling a little better, Staci took a nap.

Amber never left her side.

Chapter 20

"Morning, Cook," said Nathan entering the kitchen.

"Morning," said Cook.

Nathan looked around the kitchen. It seemed different this morning. Then he spotted it, on the far wall where the helpers cut the vegetables and kneaded the bread. It was a painting of a family by an old shed.

"I've never seen that picture before," said Nathan.

"What picture?" asked Cook intent in her sauce making by the stove.

"The old one of the family standing in front of a shed."

Cook stiffened. She shut off the stove. She turned to the wall where Nathan was looking, a pained expression grew on her face. She walked over to the painting, took it off the wall and walked out the back door. Nathan followed.

"What did I say wrong?" asked Nathan.

"Nothing," said Cook.

"What are -"

"I'm getting rid of it," said Cook.

"Why?"

"I can't talk about that."

Nathan stopped following and watched Cook put the picture in the dumpster and slam the lid. She seemed angry now and didn't look at Nathan as she walked past him back to the kitchen. Nathan followed her back into the kitchen where she resumed her cooking.

Nathan waited for Cook to explain. She remained silent. Nathan went to the counter to get his breakfast and sat at a table in the dining room.

Later that day Nathan went to the dumpster to find the picture. The garbage cans were empty. He walked into the dark kitchen. It was not on the wall.

As Nathan grabbed a banana to take to his room, Cook entered.

"Why did you get rid of the picture?" asked Nathan.

Cook looked tired. "I don't need it anymore. It reminds me of sad things."

Nathan nodded and left Cook alone in the kitchen. Going up the stairs he remembered Henry saying he didn't like to remember his old life because it stole his happiness. Then he realized that asking was not always a good idea because sometimes asking made people remember.

Chapter 21

It rained and thundered for two straight days. By the second day Nathan couldn't stand it. It was the first time that it had rained since he had arrived at the ranch. At first, he was surprised, because, somehow, he thought that the ranch always had nice weather. But, of course, that was silly. It had to rain once in a while, otherwise all the trees would die.

That second day of rain seemed to wear on other people too. The mood was subdued, but not glum. Nathan started to feel just a little claustrophobic, not seeing the sun and the constant drip of water from the eaves onto his windowsill. The short bursts of thunder and lightning were invigorating, but the rain made Nathan feel wet and cold all the way to the bone. The living room seemed to get bigger as everyone came to sit and enjoy the fire. Nathan was working the fireplace most of the day.

At dinner, the dining room fireplace was lit, and the room was packed with people playing cards, board games and joking. The seldom-used kitchen fireplace was lit and going, and some braved the jostling of the kitchen staff to stand by its blaze.

Nathan asked Cook about the weather and why everyone was so quiet.

"The old man is in his deep waiting," said Cook.

"Deep waiting. What is that? What does the rain

have to do with the old man?" asked Nathan.

"It's time to pray," said Cook. "Someone is in a bad place and the Seekers are trying to find him. Or maybe they have found him and it's too late. Or maybe they've found him, and he doesn't want to return. Maybe it's something else."

"Who is it?"

"It doesn't matter, Child," said Cook. "Just pray."

Nathan stood looking at Cook.

Cook noticed. "You never pray before?"

"I don't know."

"Well, you just think about the lost person, and you think about the old man, and you imagine the best thing happening and the lost person coming home, coming over that grassy knoll, coming out and we seein' him and cheering, and the old man runnin' out to meet him and the huggin'. You think about that and ask for it to happen."

Nathan sort of understood.

"Go read chapter 12 of the book," said Cook going back to cleaning.

Nathan felt dismissed.

"You ain't bothering me. I'm just in the prayer kinda way, is all."

"Okay," said Nathan, feeling relieved. "See you tomorrow."

"Good night, Child. Remember what I said."

Back in his room Nathan curled up in his chair and read chapter 12. All the guilt and fear faded away.

Cook was right. She must have memorized this book, he thought.

He closed his eyes and listened to the quiet bird song floating in through his wet, cracked-open windows. He imagined Joe walking over the hill and getting a hug from the old man.

He knew he might never actually see it happen but praying really helped.

The rain lifted. The clouds broke. Orange light

from the setting sun streamed in through his window. He imagined Joe smiling. He smiled to himself. It seemed like Cook was always right.

Chapter 22

The next day Nathan asked Cook about Staci. Cook said she was working with the kitchen staff and was getting good at chopping vegetables.

"She's been through a lot, Nate. You may want to take it really slow with her."

"Okay, Cook," Nathan said. "But I'll say 'Hi' when I see her."

"Oh, yes. You don't want to be rude."

Nathan decided to take a day to walk farther on the grounds. He was learning who he was, and he really didn't want to remember the pain, the fights, the nasty comments, and the unrealistic expectations his birth father had had for him. It still irked him that he hadn't heard from his father at all. Maybe he didn't know where Nathan was. That was okay by him.

Nathan walked out the front door, down the porch and in the opposite direction of the Castle. He really wanted to see the Castle again, but something told him it wasn't a good idea.

He could see the other side of the stables, the training track, the fenced pasture, the meadow beneath scattered oaks, maples, and pine trees.

Soon, in the distance, he could see a tall stone building. Perhaps this was another Castle, or another school.

Nathan followed a wide path that led toward the

strange building out in the meadow. A few trees shaded the path along the way with benches for sitting and an occasional picnic table.

Nathan came to a bridge wide enough for two big trucks to pass, but there were no tire tracks. Nathan stood in the middle of the bridge. Along the banks of the river he saw gentle slopes, rocky banks, and sandy beaches. In places the river was dark blue reflecting the white clouds. Nathan wondered if this was the same river he taken a drink from on their trip to the New Building.

Crossing the bridge Nathan made his way past herb and flower gardens. Windows in the building were open and Nathan could hear voices. It was a choir singing a song he had heard somewhere before. This song felt safe and calming to him.

As he approached the large church, he heard a service. The choir was singing another song he recognized but could not name. He thought he heard instruments as well.

Suddenly Nathan became aware of what he was wearing. He looked down at his ratty tennis shoes, his jeans with a hole in one knee (he really needed to patch those) and his t-shirt with the grass stain (time to do laundry). He sniffed his shirt and looked at his not-quite-clean hands and made the move to leave.

"Please. You can stay," said a deep voice to his right. "No one here cares what you look like or how you smell."

Nathan looked at the man welcoming him. He was tall, thin, with bushy white-hair, and a long white beard. He was slightly bent over and leaned on a thick, intricately carved walking stick.

Nathan smiled and nodded. The ancient man motioned him to go in. Nathan suddenly remembered his manners. "I'm Nathan," he said.

"My name is Hamilton."

"Nice meeting you, Hamilton," whispered Nathan.

"And you, Nathan – You can call me Methuselah … everyone does. I guess I'm the oldest one here at the ranch." At this the ancient man laughed in a quiet, coarse wheeze. "Welcome to the Old Stone Gathering Place."

Nathan didn't want to go in, but he did. There was scratchy sandpaper in his chest. He never liked church. It always smelled like strong old lady perfume and guilt. He sat in the empty back pew.

The vaulted pine ceilings were carved in scrolling patterns of many layers, unpainted and polished. The beams above were thick and strong, crossing back and forth creating a dance of light and shadow on the people, the walls, the windows, the pews, the floor. The choir's song lifted his heart though he didn't know the words. The melody died away and echoed through the building and the sandpaper in his chest was gone.

There were readings and things shared, like speeches and storytelling. Nathan listened intently and did not notice when Methuselah took a seat across the aisle.

Then the service was over. Nathan came back to himself and tensed for the inevitable barrage of questions from everyone else in attendance and the promises he would have to make to return every Sunday forever and ever.

But that didn't happen. A few people smiled at him, and some shook his hand.

Nathan stayed where he was, just thinking, enjoying the beauty of the building and the sun's rays moving so slowly and the artwork on the walls and the designs of tile on the floor. He felt content.

The large stained-glass mosaic window at the front let in the colored sunlight. Each piece of glass seemed to move. New pieces appeared flowing in and out like liquid. Nathan was mesmerized.

After a long while, Nathan got up to leave.

"Each piece of glass represents a member of the

community," said Methuselah, "someone who lives and works at the ranch. Their piece stays even if they leave or die. The pieces move around to create a new work art."

Then he smiled, "Nice to meet you, Nathan. You are welcome here anytime, day or night."

"Night? You're open at night too?" said Nathan.

"People need comfort at all hours. Why should a place of comfort be closed?"

"But people are so happy here. I don't understand."

"Are you happy?"

"I guess so," said Nathan studying the floor.

"Are you content with your room, your assignments, your friends?"

"Yes, but sometimes I think there must be more for me to do, more to life."

"Have you made peace with your old life?"

"What do you mean," Nathan asked, memorizing the diagonal pattern at his feet.

"Do you know where you came from?"

"Yes."

"Does it worry you that you didn't say 'Good-bye'?" Methuselah's questions came slowly, carefully. "Does it make you angry or sad that the family and friends from your old life haven't tried to come and get you?"

"Maybe."

"Nathan, I must tell you something important," said Methuselah, putting his hand on Nathan's shoulder. "You can call me a crazy old man, and many do, but I know this to be the truth. There is a war coming and you will have to fight in this war. You will have to choose a side and it will not be an easy decision."

"What do you mean," Nathan asked. "How do you know there's going to be a war? Everything here is so – so peaceful."

"I have lived a very long time. I have seen many wars. I have seen this building burned, riddled with bullets and the windows broken with stones. I know Ken well and we speak often. He chose you for a very important job. He sent Joe to get you so that you could be part of this ranch, so that you could be prepared. He knew he was taking a risk, but he trusts you. He trusts your heart. There is a war coming and it will happen soon, in fact, things are beginning to happen around the borders of this expansive place of which many are not aware. Soon you will hear distant gun fire and the Rest House, and the secret places will be filled with the casualties. Ken has fought many wars and he has been preparing for this war since the last one ended.

"We have had many years of peace, but we have seen the signs. Phil Amor covets this land. It makes no sense, of course. He is already a very rich man beyond imagining, but I believe he has the dark heart of a conqueror, and he will not stop until he owns the entire nation – or he dies.

"I do not want to see another war. Perhaps you will be instrumental in preventing it. Perhaps Ken saw from the beginning that you were the key."

Nathan nodded. He didn't know what to say. He was nobody. He didn't know how to fight. He didn't care about being rich. But he did care about the old man sitting on the front porch and he did care about this ancient man as well. He cared about Henry and Sam and Solomon and Cook and Staci and all the others. He didn't want to see them hurt.

He walked away from Methuselah toward the front of the great room and studied the artwork on the walls and the windows imagining how it must have been when the building had been broken. Something was growing inside of him, and he didn't understand it, but he knew he had to go talk to the old man.

He walked back to Methuselah to thank him, but the ancient man was gone.

Back at the Big House the old man was not on the front porch. Nathan went to his room without talking to anyone. He sat in his comfy chair which seemed more comfortable than ever. He finished reading the dusty blue book which was more interesting somehow.

Then he went to find the old man again.

Out on the porch, the old man was talking to Sam about the old days. Sam was remembering a battle in the war and the day his horse got wounded. His commander wanted to shoot the beast, but Sam begged him not to. It worked out in the end. The leg healed and the horse was ride-able within a year.

"Hi, Nate. How are things?" said Sam.

"Good, Sam. Good to see you. Saw you yesterday at lunch."

"Missed you. Sorry, Nate. Let's see, yesterday at lunch, was I with the gang?"

"The gang?"

"Yeah. Solomon, Henry, Miles and Chef."

"I guess so." Nathan sat down on a chair away from the men and waited. Now they were talking about preparations, strategic encampments, ammunition, supplies, and staff. This made Nathan's stomach churn with butterflies as the words of the ancient one echoed in his ears.

Nathan got up to do his sweeping. Cleaning always cleared his head.

He tried to set the ancient words aside and trust the old man's timing.

Chapter 23

Henry and Sam woke Nathan early the next day before sunrise. They made their own breakfast in the dark kitchen. Henry was a pretty good cook. Fried eggs, hash browns, sausage, toast. They ate quickly, cleaned up and packed a lunch.

They had work to do.

"We can't wait anymore, Nate," said Sam. "You need to be trained."

"And now," said Henry.

They moved to the stables and saddled up. The old war horse was stomping and ready. Kane whinnied at the sight of Nathan. They moved between a trot and a lope, making good time through the meadow, the gardens, the orchards and down the trail to the dry wash.

"Are we going out to the New Building?" asked Nathan.

"Yup," said Sam. "They're ready to go. The other outposts are farther away and just got started."

"We will need to go to all of them," said Henry. "We don't know where they will hit first. You need to know where they all are."

"Phil Amor?" asked Nathan.

"Yup," said Henry. "And his crew. They're all trained mean. No integrity. No conscience. Don't know how they keep things going."

"Money," said Sam.

"Yeah," answered Henry. "Money is a pretty powerful motivator. He gets guys that are down on their luck, right out of jail, unemployed, homeless, then offers them a bundle as sign on. He runs a hard business."

The rest of the day was spent on the shooting range, the training arena, and the new meeting room reading maps of the ranch and the outlying areas. Nathan was surprised at how large the ranch was. He was tired by dinner time. His finger and thumb hurt from loading ammo into magazines. His legs were shaky from alternately kneeling and standing for long periods of time. His back ached from being on his feet. He was exhausted and hungry and had never felt better in his entire life.

"You're a quick study," said Sam. "That's good."

"Nothing replaces experience," said Henry, concentrating on his food.

"Well, we don't have that luxury, now, do we," said Sam, just a little on edge.

Henry grunted, then perked up a bit. "Remember, Nate, you don't want to be gut-shot. That's a slow painful death, unless there's a good surgeon close by. Being as how we'll be stationed at one of the outposts, having a surgeon might not be an option."

Nathan felt a chill run all through him. Suddenly it was all just a little more real.

"Never underestimate your enemy," said Sam. "Always assume he's stronger than you, has more guns than you, more horses, more ammo, more men, and more resources than you. And always assume he knows where you are. Leave nothing to chance."

"Sounds like something my father would say," said Nathan.

The men were silent. Nathan squashed the urge to apologize.

After the food kicked in, Henry asked, "Did you get training when you lived, ah, over there?"

"I don't know," said Nathan. "I remember living in town. I don't remember much about the ranch."

"Are you sure," asked Sam. "Because you could have fooled me today. You shot a 90 percent, revolver and rifle, and we only had to adjust your grip a bit. You've handled firearms before."

"Maybe he's just a quick study, Sam," commented Henry.

"I don't remember," said Nathan. "I guess I still have a lot of holes in my memory."

"Do you remember any of your schooling?" asked Henry.

"Yeah. A little. When I was in the school house once I had a flash of a memory, but that was when I was little, like maybe six or seven."

"You remember graduating?"

"Nope."

"Well, it's okay if it don't come," said Henry. "I'm glad we have you with us. You have been a big help."

Nathan muttered a thank you.

"If you ask me, your blood dad is a fool," announced Sam. "Maybe he ain't really your blood dad."

No one commented on that. Soon the other men were coming in from their work and preparations, sitting at surrounding tables. The happiness and comradery were tainted by the stress of impending battle.

"Many of these men fought in the last war," said Sam.

"Who was the enemy?" asked Nathan.

"Does it matter?" asked the man.

"It was a man named Cole," said Sam, trying to keep things light. "He had a tiny ranch south of here. But the war started the same as this one. A few lost sheep that we found out later were stolen. A few cattle roaming on our land with the wrong brand -"

"Or one of ours that'd been tampered with," said another.

"An employee dead or taken to the Rest House," said still another.

Now the talk was of memories of past wars, successful battles, men shot down, men who survived, horses that were valiant in the middle of a skirmish. Then the conversation moved on to good tactics, how some things worked, and some things didn't. Nathan soaked it all in and tried to keep fear at bay.

"Does the old man still fight?" asked Nathan. The room went quiet. Nathan felt awkward as if he had said a string of foul words.

"Shem? You want to take this one?" called Henry across the room.

"Sure," said Shem. A tall, broad-shouldered man strode over to Nathan's table. Henry made room for him.

"Make no mistake, the old man is excellent with a gun," said Shem, "and a horse, unraveling battle tactics, everything a good general should be. But the old man is also the center. Let me explain. He's responsible for everything and everybody. He knows who is the best and at what, who to call when there's trouble, where the safest places are, where the hidden places are, and what everybody is doing every minute of the day."

Nathan shook his head thinking what Shem had just said was impossible.

"You don't have to believe me, but you must understand how things work. If the old man were here in the fight, we would lose the center, the headquarters. There would be a breakdown in communication and supplies and support and food and intelligence and health and everything else. He must do what he does so we can do what we do."

Shem paused and waited for someone else to add. No one spoke up so he went on.

"I was here during the last range war. The old man came out to one of the fights out on the south end of the ranch." The crowd was quiet now, listening to Shem's memory of a fight most of them had been in.

Some were nodding their heads in agreement. "I fought in the small group he was in. We were able to fight them back over the border. Suddenly, the old man went ghost-white and yelled, 'the Rest House! We must protect the Rest House!' By the time our group arrived, the Rest House was engulfed in flames. Cole's men had found their way past the west border patrol, and they were able to do a lot of damage."

"We lost twelve men," said one.

"Edom Cole lost more," said Shem.

"But we were able to stop them from hitting the Big House," said another. "Cole lost everything. Amor bought the Cole place after that ... like the vulture he is."

"Since that day," said Shem, "The old man has stayed where he is – at the center. The rest of the war lasted one week. That was because he was able to take in information from the outside, from all the outposts and let everyone else know what was going on and what was needed."

Nathan was quiet. He understood and was nodding along with some of the others. Nathan was beginning to understand that to question was acceptable, but the go against orders was just plain stupid. Everything had been worked out from the beginning.

Nathan spoke up. "You mentioned the Hiding Places ..."

"Yes," said Shem. "We have many hiding places that are safe places to go if you are wounded or hurt or even lost. We will show you some tomorrow and you can see them all on the map. I hear you're good with maps."

Nathan shrugged.

It was getting dark.

"Best get a little rest," said Sam. "We'll be doing some night work."

"Remember," said Henry, "if you're in trouble, pray."

Nathan nodded. He found an empty cot and fell asleep to the rise and fall of conversation. There were other newbies in their ranks asking questions. Nathan felt better about that and hoped to meet them all. But for now he was sticking close to Henry and Sam.

Chapter 24

Nathan slept longer than he should. But looking for Henry and Sam, he realized with a twist in his middle that he was in a strange tent.

He was lying on his back on a cot with a headache. The tent was large and warm, comfortable, with chairs and tables and places to store things and even a desk. He tried to get up, but pain exploded behind his left ear. He closed his eyes and wished for it to pass.

As it subsided, he stared up at the top of the tent, brown and worn, and tried to remember how he got there. At first, he thought he had been taken to one of the other outposts as he slept, even though that didn't seem possible.

He heard voices outside, but none that he recognized. Then he heard a voice that chilled his bones – his father. An explosion of memory hit his heart, the failures, the beatings, the long sermons, and all the reasons he had run away from home.

With a painful flash he remembered awakening and saddling up, the late-night ride to another outpost on Kane, losing track of Henry and Sam in the dark, the scuffling in the bushes near the orchards, hands and arms grabbing him and a wet cloth closing over his mouth and nose.

"You better not have damaged him," said the

stern, tenor voice, approaching the tent. Nathan quickly turned away from the entrance to the tent and covered his head with the blanket. Fear and anger pounded in his heart. He wished he could make himself invisible.

He heard boots entering the tent. He heard his father's familiar huff, the one he heard a million times if he were sleeping in, late, sick, hurt, or if he had failed in any way. Dread replaced fear. Then anger replaced dread. The boots turned and walked out.

"Give him another hour, then wake him. I can't wait all day."

"Yes, Sir." That voice, where had he heard it before. A spark of recognition followed by another wave of fear – Joe. So Joe had turned enemy. After a moment of regret at putting his trust in an untrustworthy person, Nathan felt pity for Joe. He knew his father had mastered the art of getting people to do his bidding. He was a brutal man and if Joe hadn't been beaten yet, it was only a matter of time.

Nathan worked on an escape plan, but realized, knowing Phil Amor, he didn't stand a chance. On the other hand, Sam and Henry had taught him a lot. Maybe he could make it. On still another hand, if he failed it was certain he would experience great pain and humiliation.

He could see the feet of the guards or whoever they were in the tiny slit of light where the tent met the ground. There seemed to be regular intervals where each of the pairs of boots moved positions around the tent. With a sinking heart Nathan decided to wait it out. Maybe they'd tell him why he had been kidnapped.

Kidnapped. He wasn't a kid. And he wasn't really napped since Phil Amor was his real father. Nathan sat up. The pain now a dull ache. A couple of aspirin would really be good about now, he thought.

He remembered the day he met Joe. He was sitting in his favorite diner in town waiting for life to begin, wishing he was someplace else, hoping he could move even farther away and escape the family obligation of taking over the business so his father could travel. He had run away, but his family had found him. His father had left him in town to fend for himself - "It'll teach you a lesson," he had said. He still couldn't remember how old he was. But Joe had shown up, bought a burger and asked him if he was – was – his head ached more as he tried to remember his given name.

"Ethan." His father stood in the tent doorway. He moved his head but couldn't see him well because of the back light. Nathan braced himself.

"Ethan, we've missed you," said his father obviously trying to sound loving which ended up sounding comical.

Nathan replayed his training, his preparing.

"I need you, Ethan. I'm sorry for the rough treatment, but we needed to get you out before the fighting started."

"Fighting," Nathan croaked.

"Yes, Ethan, it's not about land, it's about you. They stole you from me. They must pay."

Nathan suddenly saw his father in a new light. Phil Amor really wasn't his father anymore. The old man on the porch was his father now. The old man cared for him, gave him advice, let him make decisions on his own and work at his own pace.

This man calling himself his father was something else now. This man wanted to take over the ranch and steal all the things that the old man had worked so hard for. This man was his enemy and probably always had been. This man wanted to use him for his own ends. He was a manipulator, an intimidator and at the worst of times, a dominator.

The old man and all his friends, all the people that cared for him, listened to him, taught him – they were his family.

And right then, in that moment, Nathan made a choice. He would have to fight. But in the back of his mind he heard Sam saying, "Fight smart. Know your enemy. Wait patiently for your chance. Prepare your next three moves. Be alert."

Nathan did not want to give this man any more reason to be evil than he already had. He thought about the old man. He said a short prayer in his head.

Somehow, he felt a tiny bit of hope forming in the front of his brain. Maybe there was a way out. He would wait and bide his time. Nathan smiled.

"What's so funny?" asked Phil.

"Nothing is funny. I just know who you are."

"Oh? Who am I?"

"You are the enemy," Nathan said, slowly and deliberately, with as little emotion as possible. "You want to take Ken's ranch away from him and everyone who has worked so hard to make it what it is. You are a thief. You only want to steal, kill and destroy."

Instantly, as it is with second nature, Phil lifted his hand to slap Nathan hard. Nathan was ready, his arm swung up to block the blow. Phil stopped himself. Then he laughed.

"You got yourself some courage while you were away, I see. Interesting. You are even more valuable to me now than you were when they took you."

"They didn't take me," said Nathan standing to face Amor, ignoring the pain in his head. "I left. I wanted to leave. Remember? I ran away. I was tired of all the abuse. I wanted you to let me alone, I wanted your so-called friends to leave me alone, but I guess your spies found me – or should I say, Joe found me?"

"You were always an ungrateful boy," Phil said raising his voice. "What I did, I did for your own good. You were too soft. You needed to be tough, so I made you tougher. We fed you the best food, dressed you in the best clothes, took you to all the cultural events and educated you in the best schools. Well, you will have some value yet for me. I need return on my investment."

Nathan didn't ask what that would be. He

couldn't remember any best school or cultural event. But it didn't matter. He looked down at the dirt floor and waited for the conversation to end.

"Sir, it's time," said Joe from just outside the tent entrance.

"Thank you, Joe. Join me, Ethan. There is something I need to show you."

Nathan steadied himself, his head still foggy. He followed Phil out of the tent and into the bright sun. All around were tents and horses and trucks. He searched for places to hide. Phil walked him to a ridge where he could see the New Building in the distance. As he studied the scene, he saw a group of riders – mere pinheads on the meadow – moving toward the New Building. Amor's camp was just on the border of The Ranch.

Nathan pulled out his mirror to signal by reflecting light from the sun.

Quickly, Phil slapped it out of his hand. The mirror crashed in pieces on the rocks.

Then, gun shots, tiny pops from far away.

The war had begun.

Chapter 25

Nathan spun around and ran in the opposite direction. He had to get a horse. He had to help them. He had been trained for this moment. He dodged between tents and spotted tethered steeds.

He heard Amor call out. From somewhere behind him and a group of men grabbed and held him. He struggled. Amor approached him.

Nathan looked Amor in the eyes and said, "I will not fight for you. Those people down there are my family."

Amor slapped Nathan hard on the cheek. He brushed passed the crowd and disappeared behind the tents. He came back with a shot gun. The men smiled knowing what he was going to do. Two held him by the arms and the rest spread out. Amor aimed at Nathan's middle. Henry's words came to him, "You don't want to be gut-shot. That's a slow painful death, unless there's a good surgeon close. If not, use your pistol to finish the job."

They had taken his pistol.

Nathan stood straight and waited for it to come.

"Well, boy, aren't you going to beg?" sneered one of the men watching.

Nathan kept his eyes on Amor.

"You're just a bloody coward," said another.

The interchange seemed ludicrous to Nathan, like

a conversation that didn't involve him, as if they were talking about someone else, as if he were watching the scene in a movie. He knew the next move was his father's. If he got shot, so be it. If he didn't, and he didn't think he would, why would he have been kidnapped anyway? Perhaps now would be the time that Amor would give him specifics. Or, maybe, he just wanted to inflict more emotional pain. Nathan steeled himself against the verbal abuse. Somehow, he knew the old man knew where he was, and it gave him an inner strength he had never known before.

"You were never much good as a son," Amor said. Yep. There it was. So predictable. Nathan tried not to smile. "Don't you have anything to say?"

"No, Sir," said Nathan.

"I don't get you. I should shoot you right now, but I think the old man would pay a pretty penny to have you back," said Amor.

Nathan kept watching him. There was something else there. Something Amor was struggling with. A veil seemed to fall over his face. Was it emotion? Was it some distant pin prick of light that could be called "love?" Maybe Amor didn't know what to do when people weren't begging him for mercy. Maybe he was trying to think up another argument to get Nathan to talk. Maybe he didn't want to be embarrassed in front of his men.

"I tried to train you right, son," said Amor. "But you just wouldn't learn. I blame it on your mother. Your mother kept you soft." The hardness returned to his eyes and Nathan thought, now he will shoot me.

Suddenly shots rang out from all around the camp. Nathan was dropped like a hot potato as everyone rushed to their stations. There was yelling, return fire, tents going down, horses clamoring, and dust kicking up. He crawled under a truck. Phil Amor spit out a quick, "Stay here!" and ran to the action. Nathan was alone. "Stay here?" he said to himself quietly, amused. "Is he talking to me?"

Nathan crawled out and rushed to an outcropping of rock below the camp to hide behind and to think. He was sure he knew some of the men that attacked the Amor camp. Amor had set up just outside the boundary of the ranch and a group Nathan had trained with were among those assigned to attack it. He had to get a weapon. What had they done with his pistol?

Nathan moved around, running low from cover to cover. Suddenly he spotted Jake, the leader of the northern outpost. He held back the urge to call out. He was on the wrong side of the battle without a weapon. He worked his way steadily downhill behind rocks with his back to the cliff side and on his belly.

The shots were down to an occasional outburst of three or four. Everyone was hunkered down. The timid were staying put. The bravest of each side were inching in the direction of the enemy.

Nathan reached an open area. He felt the sharp sting as a bullet singe his left arm. He dove back to cover. Moving up slowly, he saw Jake. Jake spotted him as Nathan sank down to ground level. The shooting lessened as each side tried to save ammo.

Then, Nathan decided it was time to take a chance. He made a run for it in the direction of Jake. Jake saw it coming and stood to shoot. Nathan jumped to the ground thinking Jake was aiming at him, but he wasn't. A moment later he heard a grunt as a shooter behind him went down.

"Nate," Jake yelled out.

Nathan ran to the rocky shelter into which Jake had disappeared. He jumped into the brush just as a bullet caught him below the knee. He yelped in pain. Jake pulled him farther in behind the rocks.

"Where are we?" asked Nathan. Jake and another man explained where they were according to the original plans they had studied. The other man tied up Nathan's leg and arm.

"You're out of it, Kid," said Jake.

"No!" said Nathan. "I want to fight."

"You got guts kid, but the old man wants you alive. I think Amor wants you alive, too."

"Could have fooled me," said Nathan bitterly.

"We came to get you," said the other man.

"How did you know where I was?" Nathan asked.

"Got a call from the old man," said Jake.

Suddenly it was raining bullets. Jake went down. Nathan scrambled to get Jake's shot gun. He told Jake to lay still and he took his spot. The barrage came from the new group – reinforcements. Nathan was shooting at anything in the enemy's direction that moved. Then another barrage from another direction father away on the other side of the camp.

Nathan smelled weeds burning, then the acrid smell of rubber burning, then the scream of horses and men yelling. Someone had set fire to the Amor camp. Jake called out. Nathan looked him over. It was his shoulder. Nathan grabbed a rag from a nearby sack and wrapped it the best he could. He wished now that he would have learned something from the healers. He could be using it right now. He heard truck tires on gravel. Amor's crew was pulling out to attack somewhere else.

"Jake! You okay?" Nathan asked.

"I think I passed out. I think it's just my shoulder. I'll try and get up in a minute ... I'm missing it. We need to get up there and make the capture and let the horses go."

"Capture? asked Nathan.

The shooting had stopped. Jake was moving again. Nathan joined Jake on moving up the hill to the camp. They found the horses and untied them. The horses took off down the hill in the direction of the New Building. "Most of them are ours!" yelled Jake.

They moved to the other side of the camp and found more men from the ranch finishing the job of rounding up the enemy and putting out the blaze. Phil

Amor was not among them. Somehow Nathan was not surprised.

Henry yelled at Nathan, "Check all the tents. We need to find anyone who's left."

Nathan joined the others in the search. He found a horse caught near a burning tent. He freed it, taking off its halter. He did the best he could looking in the burning tents, calling out to make sure no one was inside. He felt blood trickle down his leg and tried not to think about it.

He heard a noise in the next tent and looked in. There was someone tied up on a chair. He pulled out his knife and started in on the ropes. The girl was struggling and yelling at him.

"Calm down. I'm trying to get you out of here before you burn!" he said.

"Leave me alone!" she yelled.

Nathan stopped and looked at her face.

It was Staci. She was black and blue.

"You want to stay here? Fine!" yelled Nathan in frustration. "But I have my orders." This time he wasn't gentle, just business. He got the ropes cut and off. Staci made for the door.

"Staci!" yelled Nathan.

"You're with the enemy! I heard! They said you were Phil Amor's son!"

Nathan couldn't argue with that. As he escaped the tent, he saw Staci had run over to where Sam and Henry were waiting. Nathan grabbed her by the arm.

"Wondered what happened to you, Staci," said Henry, looking beat right down to his socks as he liked to say at the end of the day. "Nate, she was kidnapped about the same time you were."

"Henry!" yelled Staci, "Don't trust him! He's Phil -"

"Phil Amor's son, yep, we know. Let her go, Nathan. She's gonna do what she feels is right."

Nathan let her go. She turned on him and slapped him in the face – hard enough to make his ears ring.

When she tried to slap him again, Nathan caught her arm in mid-slap. She pulled away and stomped off down the hill.

"She'll come around," said Sam. "Just give her some time. She's confused."

"I'm just hoping she doesn't shoot me," Nathan said with a half-smile.

Sam let out a weak laugh, floundered with his gun, and went down on his knees.

"Sam!" Nathan rushed over to help.

"Sam, we got to get you to the Rest House," said Henry.

"You better be comin' with me, old timer," said Sam, trying to laugh.

Chapter 26

Three days later, Nathan was well enough to leave the Rest House, albeit with a slight limp. He went down the hall to visit Henry and Sam first.

"Got to stay another week, Nate," said Henry. "I guess I'm getting too old to ride and shoot and crawl around on my belly in the prickly brush."

Nathan was disappointed, but glad Henry was doing better. The diagnosis had been heat exhaustion and dehydration.

Nathan said good-bye to Henry and walked over to the next bed to see Sam. As he suspected, Sam had been grazed by a bullet on his left rib cage during the shooting. Sam said he had at least another two weeks, maybe more.

"I'll visit you every day," said Nathan.

"It's okay if you don't," said Sam. "You'll have things to do now that you're well."

"You need to practice your shooting," said Henry. "Amor's not done yet."

"You might be called to another outpost," said Sam. "Don't worry. We'll hear about it."

"We have our sources," chuckled Henry.

As Nathan left the room, Henry said, "Remember, Nate, the healers said not to talk about what happened out there. We talked it to death yesterday and it's time to get ready for the next thing."

Nathan nodded and waved.

Nathan was glad to get back to his room. He lay down on his bed and stared at the ceiling, feeling completely calm, except for the tiny prick that felt like there was something left undone, someone he needed to talk to.

He thought about Staci. It wasn't Staci. He didn't know where Staci was, and he didn't want to get in an argument or get slapped again. It wasn't Cook. He didn't need to talk to Hamilton. He thought about all the people he had met since he came to the ranch searching his mind.

Then he closed his eyes and thought about the fight and getting shot, which wasn't as bad as he thought it would be. He played the scene over and over in his mind, trying to think up ways he could have done better.

Sam said he had been shot many times – "too many to count." Henry said that was an exaggeration. The healers joked that Sam was telling the truth and that Henry was just jealous. The three had gotten together the day after the fight – with permission – and discussed what was done wrong and what was done right during the taking of the enemy camp. After that they were not allowed to discuss the battle – it impeded the process of healing.

Nathan knew he shouldn't, but he played the day over in his mind. Suddenly his leg started throbbing and anger grew inside. He wanted revenge. He knew he should forgive his father, but he felt he needed to cause him pain. That is when he remembered.

He needed to talk to the old man about what Phil Amor had told him.

Nathan got up out of bed and walked down to the front porch. It was empty. The determination he had built up inside fell out. His anger grew. He stood on the top step for a minute not knowing what he should do next. He looked out over the front lawn and the huge old trees and the grassy field that led to the rest of the world. He wondered what it was like being the old man sitting on the porch watching for people to come work at the ranch, watching for people he missed, watching for family members that got angry and walked out the back door, knowing everything that was going on and making decisions that made some people happy and other people mad.

"Good morning, Nathan!" said the old man. Nathan snapped out of his contemplation and saw him sitting in his usual seat. How could he have missed him sitting there?

"Oh! Good morning, Sir," said Nathan.

"You look lost in thought."

"I was just thinking about what it would be like to be you."

"Really? What did you come up with?"

Nathan laughed a little, "I don't want to be you."

The old man chuckled.

After a moment Nathan asked. "How old are you?"

"I've been around a long, long time..."

"As long as Methuselah?"

"Longer."

"Longer? But he's so old. You can't be older than he is."

"People age in different ways. We age in our bodies, yes. But we also age in our minds and in our souls. Have you heard people call someone an old soul?"

"Yes. That's someone who is really nice, right? Or really wise?"

"Yes and no. Being an old soul for some means they have great understanding. They know just what to say at just the right time. They know how to listen in a way that alleviates other people's pain. They seem to know what to do in all situations or they can question others in such a way as to bring out understanding in them without humiliating them. But for others, being an old soul means having had another life, as if the knowledge and understanding gained in one life is transferred to the next. You bring your knowledge and experience from your old life to this one."

"Which one is it?"

"Well, you must decide that for yourself. If you reread the book, the last few chapters, that might help you decide which way is right for you."

"What about you?"

"Oh, I think we must make the most of this life and not depend upon the possibility of another life in another place with other people. Or hope we get another crack at knowledge and wisdom. I'll let you in on a little secret. If I knew there was going to be another life, I'd get lazy in this one."

Nathan nodded.

The old man continued. "There is a lot we can do to take care of our bodies and make them last as long as possible. But in the case of many people, like Sam, for instance, they have been wounded in battle so many times that it is as much as they can do to remain alive. Yet, if you think about Sam's attitude, he seems much younger than he really is. And that is where the mind comes in."

"Oh, like you can convince yourself you feel better than you actually do?"

"Yes, but it's much more than that. You must find the strength, courage, and perseverance inside to make each new day an adventure, a challenge, and a blessing to others. That is where the mind comes in."

Nathan thought about that. People crossed between them going out to walk or work. The old man waited for the next question. It came.

"I need to know if what Phil Amor said was true."

"What did he say to you? I heard he was brutal. I'm sorry you had to go through that."

"Thank you. Yes, I think he was going to gut-shot me, but then changed his mind for some reason."

"He needs you for his plan."

"What plan?"

"I can't know what he's thinking, but I have a hunch. He knows you know this ranch. You know most of the ins and outs of how it works. You've studied the maps. That information is important to him. He wants this ranch. He wants to expand his already-vast territory. He wants to corrupt it and make it serve him. He has the spirit of Alexander the Great, of Hitler, of Caesar. He has allowed greed to run his life."

"But why can't he be happy with what he has?"

"I don't know. That's the problem. He enjoys gaining land. He feels better with people doing his bidding and being beholden to him. He has slaves, though he would deny it, of course. There are lots of different kinds of slavery and he knows how to use each person to his advantage."

"I guess I knew some of that," said Nathan. "I remembered a lot of things while he was telling me his plan to attack the New Building. I remembered how he treated my mom. He said she was weak, and she passed that weakness on to me. He said he beat her to make her tougher." Anger began to well up inside. It was hard for Nathan to breathe.

"I'm sure he completely believes he was in the right for doing what he did. A man like Phil Amor only knows hardness and lives to get better and better at it until he is the best. That, to him, is success, a way of being better than his father, who beat him."

"Did you know his father? Ah, my grandfather?"

"Yes. We had a range war with him. That was when both ranches were smaller," the old man took out his pipe, tapped it on the rocker arm, and stuffed it slowly, thinking. Nathan watched fascinated. His old hands were graceful, sure, muscular, not shaky like most old men he had known. It was as if he wasn't old at all.

"Nathaniel, I think I should tell you what transpired between your father and me. I haven't told you because I was waiting until you were grounded in our life here. You have adjusted much faster than I thought you would. I think Henry and Sam have helped."

"Yeah, they're great. I hope they get better soon."

"They will, although, I'm concerned about Sam. He pushes himself and that good old war horse of his just a bit too much. But you can't make him stop, can you? He is happiest when he has a job to do, preferably a challenge." The old man smiled at that and lit his pipe, a flash of flame, the sweet smoke drifting from the pipe, his mouth, his nose.

"Years ago," the old man continued, "a few months after your mother disappeared, I met with your father. I knew what was happening to the family over there and I had hoped I could help in some way. There was something about you that was special. I can't explain it to you right now, but I knew you were the hope of both ranches. We met at his mansion. You came down to see who I was, but your father told you to go back to your room. I could see from that short glance that you had already started to receive the beatings that had once been your mother's."

Nathan felt as if he would cry or scream or punch something. He took a deep breath steadying himself.

"I also noted from the way he treated the staff that things had gotten a lot worse since I had visited with your grandfather years earlier in the exact same house. The women who worked there looked haggard. The men were down-right mean in their face and in their attitude. I became fearful for you and your future. Either you would become brutal like your father just to survive, or you would slip away quietly like your mother. I knew I had to act, for your sake and for the future of both estates."

Nathan waited, his face getting hot, as the old man puffed on his pipe, considering his next words.

"I offered to adopt you. At first your father

laughed. Then I offered him money and he stopped laughing. When I offered him a small piece of my property that adjoined his, he thought seriously about the proposition. He offered me a drink and asked how things would work. We talked late into the night. By morning we had made a gentleman's agreement – his word against my word with a handshake – he would allow me to adopt you. I went to my lawyers and had the papers drawn up. I knew he would create some scheme to get more from me or to drop out of the agreement altogether, so I was careful.

"The next day I arrived at his house, and he had changed his mind -"

"And that's when you kidnapped me?" Nathan was on the edge of his seat.

"No," the old man took a puff and looked out over the grassy expanse as if expecting someone to come over the hill. "I had brought two of my lawyers with me and we rearranged things the way he wanted them. I made sure he signed everything and had copies before we parted ways. The plan was that I would pick you up the next week, making the transition as quick as possible."

The old man paused for a moment. Nathan waited impatiently trying to remember seeing the old man at his old house. For a moment he thought the old man had forgotten he was there.

He continued. "Chef came with me, as did Solomon and a few other Seekers. When we arrived the upstairs maid told us you were not there. I had expected that this would happen. I showed her the paperwork and told her I did not want to involve law enforcement. She closed the door. We waited. This time Phil answered the door. He said he wasn't ready. We spoke for a few more minutes and agreed the same time next week. I was sure you didn't even know we were there. I was sure he never told you."

"No, he didn't," Nathan said in a small voice.

"Adopting you cost me a very large sum, but it

was worth it – every penny – every blade of grass.”

“I'm adopted?”

“Yes.”

“You're my dad?”

“Yes,” the old man smiled, and Nathan smiled back. “I have all the paperwork and Phil Amor's signature if you would like to see it.”

Nathan stopped smiling. “But I don't remember. You never came back to get me.”

“Yes, I did, but he never let you go. I watched you. I had several of my men hire into his outfit to keep an eye on you. I couldn't kidnap you because that would be breaking the law and our agreement. I didn't want to involve law enforcement because that would make things ugly, and I didn't want to create an atmosphere of hate or distrust with you.”

“But ... all those years ...”

“Yes, Nathan, I had to wait a long time. When you came of age, I sent a Seeker to speak with you. You were living on your own in a tiny apartment you were barely able to afford. You were rebellious and angry, and you shoved him into the street, as I remember.”

“Oh, wow, I remember that. Oh, wow. I'm really sorry.”

“You're forgiven. You didn't understand. So I waited. I sent another the next year, and the next, until, finally, Joe seemed to make the connection with you. He found you in a diner, alone and depressed. He seemed to be able to say the right things. And you came with him.”

“But why did you wait so long? Why didn't you come yourself?”

"Since you were an adult, I wanted to make sure you wanted to come, of your own free will. I wanted to make sure I hadn't made a mistake and that you really were as unhappy as I knew you to be. I don't know what Phil was waiting for. He had some twisted plan that involves you, but it's beyond my knowledge.

"After you came, I called back the men who were serving Phil all those years. One of them did not want to come back. One of them didn't make it back and was shot in the back. The other three are still in the Rest House. Their sacrifice will not be forgotten."

"Oh," said Nathan. He was overwhelmed with gratitude for the men that watched over him. He was overwhelmed by the debt he would never be able to pay.

After a moment Nathan said, "So all this time you have been my dad?"

"Yes."

"And then Phil was lying to me at the enemy camp."

"Yes, he's been lying to you for a very long time."

There was silence for a long while as both were lost in thought. The robins and meadowlarks sang to their evening songs. A gentle breeze blew through the maples. The wind in the cottonwood leaves sounded like water. Someone off in the distance made a joke and there was laughter in return.

"Nathan, I want you to do something for me, please."

"Yes, anything."

"Good," said the old man. "After you have had a chance to think about these things, I would like you to go to the Rest House and work with a Listener. You probably don't think you need one, but there are things inside of you that need to come out. Things you might not even know are there. Things you have stuffed inside to survive all those years in that ugly environment. Bad things locked up inside of us have a way of coming out at the wrong time in the wrong way. I want this ranch to be happy and productive. I think I have provided everything that anyone could need. We are a solid ranch because we take care of each other and respect each other. Listeners help in the healing process. You will need a Listener. Will you go?"

"Yes," said Nathan. "I will go."

"Thank you."

Nathan stood, still a little dazed. Suddenly, he was hugging his father, and he realized, as tears poured down, that this had been his real father all along. He felt humbled and happy and sad and angry and infuriated and strangely complete all at the same time. And then he knew his new father was right. He would probably need a Listener, maybe for a long, long time.

Chapter 27

It had been a long day of preparations. The war was not over.

Henry and Sam were out of the rest house and Nathan was feeling more confident. There had been three weeks of peace. Now Nathan was tired. His thumbs hurt from filling magazines. His head was filled with memorized maps. His back was sore from long rides to the outposts. He had fallen asleep as his head hit the pillow.

The plan was for Nathan to set out on his own to the New Building and to get his orders from the commander of the outpost. Even with being nervous about traveling on the ranch alone, Nathan slept soundly.

Bang! Nathan was jerked awake. It was pitch black, but a light flashed into his room. He was up and dressing as he stumbled to the window. In the sky he saw a falling star, huge and bright. It disappeared behind the tree line followed by a flash of light and the sound of distant thunder. At first Nathan was confused. Then, in a flash of understanding, he rushed to the front porch.

"Eat," said the old man. "Cook is packing supplies. Make sure you are prepared."

"Yes, Sir," said Nathan, turning to leave. In a moment he was caught up in a hug with the old man.

He realized with a stab of fear and pain the time had come.

"You will return," said the old man.

"Yes," said Nathan, not fully understanding what the old man meant.

He met Henry and Sam at the stables. Kane was saddled and packed. Nathan helped. No one spoke. He knew the men were supposed to stay behind. He also knew they were coming with him no matter what anyone said. He wouldn't have it any other way.

The ride out was silent. Only security was out in the gardens. There were guards posted along the trail. Some were visible, dark shadows among the rows, and Nathan knew some were not visible.

Nathan had a rock in his stomach that he tried to ignore. He hoped and prayed that everyone had escaped the blast safely, but the Healers had also been packing to follow as soon as the area was secure.

Another rumble of thunder caused the three to stop. Sam pulled his war horse around to the west, then the north. Nathan followed his lead toward the bright light just fading. "They got the coordinates from someone," he said.

"Yeah," said Henry. "I think we know who."

Nathan said nothing. He knew they meant Joe. He worried the north camp had been hit, the most hidden camp and the most secure. The rock in his stomach grew.

"Watch out for spies," said Sam.

"Yeah. Nate, they all know you and they might send someone you know, someone you haven't seen for a long time. Just be careful."

"I won't give anything away," Nathan whispered.

Two more flashes lit up the northern sky.

The greenhouse was undamaged. As they passed it, his admiration for the set-up of the ranch grew. He didn't realize until that moment that wars and rumors of wars had created a specific plan for the building of the ranch. He hoped that his short time with Phil Amor had not given away any of its secrets.

Sam, leading the way, paused before coming out into the open. Henry cocked his rifle. Sam drew his ancient firearm. Nathan pulled out his pistol and readied his mind as he continued to work on ignoring that big rock in his stomach.

Henry and Sam looked at each other, then at Nathan. Nathan nodded. The three took off at a straight gallop across the flat toward the New Building.

No shots were fired. The horses were sweaty when they arrived. The early dim haze of dawn inspired hope in Nathan's heart. The building seemed unharmed. The bombs had stopped. Nathan prayed the enemy had run out of ammo. Missiles and tanks were illegal weapons after all. The unfairness of it all threatened to overwhelm the joy of the ride.

"Nate, take a ride around the perimeter before you stable your animal," ordered Sam.

"Yes, Sir," said Nathan, taking off in the opposite direction.

On the far side of the building a shadowy figure leaned against the wall. Nathan rode closer his pistol at the ready.

The woman did not belong in a ranch atmosphere in the morning haze. A spy, he thought, or a trick. Her clothes were inappropriate for outpost work, tight jeans, spike heels, low cut blouse. She wore sunglasses which were unnecessary.

He approached and studied her. "Can I help you?"

The woman let out an unladylike snort. Nathan felt a pinprick of recognition.

Against his better judgment, Nathan dismounted, but lead his horse close just in case.

"Who are you? Do you need help? Are you lost?" Nathan hoped the barrage of questions would get her to talk. He paused and searched the area around him suspecting an ambush.

He took another step toward her and was suddenly hit with a black dread like a strong wind.

"Bambi?"

At the name she smiled, her bright red lip stick sharply contrasting her flashing white teeth. He could smell her thick flowery perfume, the one she always wore, the one that made him feel stupid.

This was his father's wife, Bambi. His blood froze in his veins, and he tried to fight the nausea growing in his stomach. Memories flooded his mind. She was incredibly rude to waiters. She bought anything she wanted, then threw it away a few days later. She slapped him for talking back to her, nails cutting his face. She kicked the stray cat he had brought home. She stabbed at him with the tip of her umbrella until it hurt, claiming she was just teasing him. She was the messiest woman he had ever met, yet she complained about the state of his room or Staci's clothes strewn all over her bed. She even complained about Phil's mess – when he wasn't around.

Nathan fought the urge to run. His dread slowly ebbed away as caution and training took its place. She has no power here, he thought, no power over him, no power over anyone. But what was she doing here?

"Aren't you a little far from your castle?" asked Nathan tensing for the inevitable fight.

She smiled back at him, that evil, don't-you-want-to-kiss-me smile and said, "Why Ethan. You're all grown up. What have they been doing to you?"

"Why are you here, Bambi?"

"I think your voice changed too. How wonderful."

Nathan stopped the game. He got back on his horse to finish rounds and report the possible spy.

He met Henry coming around the other way. "Secure," said Henry.

Nathan stopped. "There's a lady on the west side of the building – Phil Amor's wife. I don't know what she's doing here."

Henry's eyes widened and yelled for Sam.

"Let's go talk to her," Henry said.

The three arrived at the spot but she was gone. Henry was not deterred. "She's up to something. Maybe she was trying to follow the crew to the hide-out. Why would they send her?"

"Or better," said Sam pulling up. "Why would she be here at all?"

"I better find her," said Nathan.

"No," said Sam. "We stick together. We go on as planned. Check the building inside and out."

Guards were stationed at each entrance only acknowledging each other with the hand sign and word of entrance – "Ichabod."

In the map room they met and exchanged information. All had made it out of the bombed north outpost. No one was hurt. The explosion had missed its target by a quarter mile, though the earth quaked and the building shook.

The three moved out towards the northwest hideout. The plan was to meet there and help out if they could. Each took a different direction to get there in case they were followed. Each direction crisscrossed the other so that tracks would confuse anyone following. Each man back-tracked the other to make doubly sure. Each man was never out of sight of another for long.

By the time they arrived the sun was bright. The same information was exchanged, the hand sign and the greeting.

Henry liked to be creative. "Hey, you guys seen Ichabod? We cain't find 'im."

"Nope," came the muffled reply, "But you can check around."

They tethered their horses in the hidden corral, then made their way through the brush into the cave.

Inside the hideout, more information was shared. No one knew where Phil Amor had gotten missiles or launchers. Several staff had been sent to report to the neighboring air force base and police stations. Phil's actions were not of a sane man, but more of a child. Why would you bomb out something you wanted to take for yourself?

Reports were coming in from the other outposts. The western outpost had also seen and felt the missile meant for the north outpost.

The eastern outpost had seen a missile hit the cotton fields. A large hole was filling with water, creating a new pond. There was no word from the southern outpost.

Chapter 28

After a bite to eat, Nathan told Henry, Sam, and the commander of the outpost that he was going to scout outside.

Henry advised him not to go alone.

Sam disagreed. "We trained him. He needs the practice." They both suspected he was going to look for Bambi.

Nathan gave himself until dinner time to search and set out in a circular scouting formation around the entrance to the hideout. This kept him moving just a bit farther out with each perimeter. It also gave him practice in walking silently, something he wasn't very good at.

The hideout was a tree covered shelter on a hill built outward from the mouth of a cave. The entrance to the hideout was hidden as well as the quarter-mile pathway leading to the entrance. There was no visible back way to get into the hideout. The entrance and pathway were lined with rocks and small alcoves where a guard could stand watch unseen.

Outside he mulled around a reason why Bambi would show up, like an evil ghost, like a nightmare. Maybe it was his imagination. Maybe he was just having a flashback. Then again, maybe she was here with other spies.

Fifteen minutes into the scout, Nathan found a

small shell casting lying near a tree. It was an odd size. He adjusted his gloves, then picked it up. After studying it he shoved it in his pocket. On the fifth go round Nathan felt himself losing his focus. He found an open area to rest. The practice was good for him, he knew that, but this was getting him nowhere. A dark veil fell over him and humiliation threatened to overwhelm him.

He was analyzing his feelings, thinking he should go back and eat something, when he heard a bird call like a whistle close by. His heart jumped. It sounded human. He was on his feet moving around the base of the hill, knowing he should go back, but not wanting to lead anyone to the hideout. He drew his pistol. He stood very still listening for a tiny rush of wind, a breaking twig, a scuff of a boot, that could signal an attack.

He inched forward.

A red rose lay 20 feet away from his position. Nathan searched as far as he could see without moving. Odd. It looked fresh and couldn't have been there for very long. He walked on as if he hadn't seen it.

"So very observant." A voice from behind jolted him. Bambi emerged from behind a tree.

Nathan froze. He felt like he wanted to run. He sure didn't want to be alone with this lady again. He was on the opposite side of the hill and the entrance so the path guards might not hear. He thought about Henry. He thought about Sam. He thought hard. Maybe they would come looking for him. Maybe he was missing dinner. He had lost track of the time.

"So talkative," she said.

He knew she wouldn't answer any of his questions. The only time she ever acted respectful was if she needed him for something.

He paused in his analyzing and thought about the old man sitting on the porch. Suddenly, he had an idea.

"Is Phil dead?" he asked loudly, hoping others would hear him.

This surprised her, but not for long. "Phil? Oh, I'm

not with him anymore."

"Finally coming to your senses," said Nathan.

"He is a cruel man."

"Is Phil dead?" he repeated, even louder.

"Oh, I don't know," Bambi said. "And I don't care." She took a step closer. Nathan caught the sickening aroma of her perfume.

"What are you doing here?" Nathan said. "Who did you come with?"

"I'm alone," she said with something new in her voice.

Nathan felt a tinge of pity. Fighting with himself he asked loudly, almost shouting, "Why did Phil send you here? Are you a spy now? Are you sneaking around in the woods, shooting whoever you find?"

The look in her eyes changed, like pain, tears dropped to her cheeks. She spread her hands open at her side as if to show she had no weapon. Nathan resisted the urge to take steps toward her, to apologize, but the pull was strong. She was crying. He hadn't ever seen her cry, not that he could remember. All he had ever seen from her was cruelty.

"Phil Amor is a brute. He beat me," this was followed by quiet sobbing.

Nathan felt his heart tear. He had never seen a mark on her, no black eyes, or dark patches on her skin (and she had shown a lot of it around the house), no limping or sudden sickness or sudden trips to the hospital. It didn't add up. She didn't even fight with Phil, at least not that he had ever heard.

"I don't believe it," said Nathan. She continued her quiet crying as if she didn't hear him. Should he wait? Should he just walk away taking a chance that she would find the hideout? Time stretched out. She couldn't be telling the truth. She was as brutal as Phil. She didn't beat people, she inflicted mental scars. He had seen her do it over and over to the staff at the house, to waiters and cashiers, to the postman. He had experienced it more times than he wanted to remember.

She was just playing him again.

"You're just as bad as he is," said Nathan angrily. "You were cruel to me, just like he was. You never said one nice word to anyone."

Her sobbing increased. "I'm sorry," she chocked. "I'm so sorry."

Nathan was split in two. He wanted to forgive her. Maybe she really had run away.

Like Nathan's mother.

"He made me … he threatened me … I had to …"

Nathan took a step toward her. A strange yearning was growing inside of him. The rose lay between them, wilting.

Nathan took another step as she wiped her eyes and looked at him. Her heavy makeup was smeared, and her face was comical. He almost laughed but stopped himself.

"Nathan," she whispered, then buried her face in her hands. She fell to her knees with fresh weeping.

Nathan moved to scoop her up. He needed to rescue her. He needed to fix her. He needed to love her. She could still be saved.

He picked up the rose on his rush to hold her and knelt in front of her. "What can I do?" he asked.

He tentatively moved his arms to touch her shoulders. She responded and slowly moved into him. Something inside Nathan exploded and he pulled her into a hug and held her close. He whispered in her ear, "What can I do?"

She sniffed, holding him a little tighter and whispered his new name, "Nathan."

The aroma, the touch, the warmth, Nathan felt himself falling. "You can … you can …" she began.

"What?" he whispered dropping the rose.

In a flash she stiffened. Her voice went cold, "You can die!"

Instantly Nathan felt a piercing hot pain in his

side. He cried out. Everything went numb. He slid sideways to the ground.

He looked at her standing over him. The evil was once again in her familiar smirk. He groped for his revolver as she turned and walked away.

Shots rang out from all around, echoing, making his ears ring. He watched as Bambi dropped in a heap to the ground next to the lifeless rose.

His last thoughts were of how stupid he had been.

Chapter 29

Back in the cave, Henry stood over Nathan watching Healers worked on his wound. They were behind room dividers made of canvas and wood. Solomon oversaw the work. Nathan was kept awake, but his eyes were closed.

Henry couldn't hold back the thoughts of failure. He had pushed Nathan too hard. Nathan wasn't ready to go out on his own. He didn't know how people like Bambi could act trustworthy while hiding a heart of stone. If Nathan died, it would be Henry's fault.

He took a sharp intake of breath, holding back unmanly tears. Nathan opened his eyes.

"Hey, Nate, you've been sleeping on the job. Didn't I teach you better?" said Henry, his voice quivering.

"Henry," Nathan squeaked, then leaned over and was sick in the pan next to his bed.

Henry grew serious. "I'll give it to ya straight, Nate. That knife she shoved in your side might have had something on it. Healers don't know what it is yet. We got some blood tests going. There was poison on the rose. Good thing you were wearing your riding gloves."

"Ah!" said Nathan as Solomon finished off the stitching.

"Finished," Solomon said. "Lie still, Nathan. So far, your vitals look good. But you will have to stay here for a while so we can watch to see how the poison is affecting your system. There might be something we couldn't find. When the local anesthetic wears off you will feel pain. I sent for Tourmaline. She will sit with you."

"Thanks, Solomon." Nathan closed his eyes and tried to relax as ordered. He had an urge to replay the scene with Bambi but knew it would bring back the initial pain. He focused his attention on imagining his body healing and relaxing. He thought of his room back in the Big House. He tried to smile.

"Heal up, Nate," said Henry moving out to make room for the Listener.

"Yes, Sir," said Nathan.

Tourmaline spoke quietly to Nathan, suggesting things he might think about, using a soothing voice to ease his mind and keep the fresh, painful memory at bay. He slept.

Tourmaline woke him an hour later. "I'm sorry, but I must wake you. We are not sure of the substance on the knife, yet. It could be a coma-inducing drug."

Nathan was groggy and tried to focus his gaze. "Okay," he croaked.

"I am Tourmaline. You may call me Malley."

"Hi, Malley," Nathan said. Malley gave him a glass of water, which he sipped.

"I must tell you what happened in the woods. You must know everything."

"Okay," said Nathan. He had been through this before after the bullet had grazed his leg.

"The lady, Bambi, has been following you for two days. She is a spy for Phil Amor. She is skilled at moving silently and at disappearing. Several of our guards engaged in conversation with her but were unable to follow her. Some think she uses witchcraft and powerful suggestion to manipulate people.

"At the New Building she was ready to kill you. One of the sentries saw she had a knife. They followed, but lost track of her after you reported speaking with her. Several of our guards here at the outpost saw her this morning. Two were sure they saw her going in the same direction as you and chose to follow her as best they could. They heard you talking loudly. There were five watching your conversation. Two called out to you as you approached Bambi for the last time. It was evident that you could not hear them. They fired when they saw she had stabbed you.

"Bambi died immediately. She had no other weapon. She was wearing a special perfume with pheromones. She also had a radio on her person for communicating. We have asked the local law enforcement for the autopsy report. The rose was quickly tested here then sent on to a lab. Preliminary tests show the stem was dipped in a poison. The knife is undergoing tests currently. We should have more information by tomorrow."

Malley waited for a moment for the events to sink in. Then she asked, "Do you have any questions?"

Nathan felt dizzy. He tried to sit up.

"Not yet," said Malley. A Healer came and propped up the head of the mattress. Nathan thanked her. "Please do not try to move," said Malley. "You might open the stitches."

Nathan nodded. Then tried to think of a question but could not.

"Do you think you could eat something?" asked Malley.

"Maybe a little," said Nathan.

A Healer brought soup. Nathan did his best to eat some of it. Suddenly he was very tired. "May I sleep again?" he asked.

"Yes, but only for a short time," said Malley. "I will be here to wake you up."

"Thank you," said Nathan, and he fell asleep.

Chapter 30

The next day, Nathan lay on his bed in the cave wishing he could be out helping. Sam came to visit Nathan before he left on his next assignment.

"Where are you going?" asked Nathan

"I can't tell you that, Nate. But I can tell you that I am going into enemy territory. I won't be alone. If we are successful, it will put an end to this war."

Nathan felt a chill in his heart. Those words made it sound like a suicide mission. He tried not to think about it.

They shook hands. Nathan watched him walk away, shaking hands with others as he went. He felt a deep foreboding. The room went quiet, and a solemn silence filled the cave.

Nathan tried to move and found that he could with only a small amount of pain. Malley was busy with others and a tiny pinprick of hope in his heart ignited an idea in Nathan's mind. He was sure the Healers would not approve so he kept it to himself. He ate more soup and took his medicine. Then he lay back and tried to sleep.

He needed rest in preparation for the execution of his plan.

Chapter 31

It was 3 a.m. and Nathan was fully awake. The air in the cave was cool and still. Everything in the cave was quiet. All he could hear was heavy breathing.

He packed up as silently as he could manage feeling only a slight twinge in his side and headed out of the cave.

He saddled up Kane. Something was happening. He could feel it in his bones.

Nathan rode in the direction of the South Outpost along the west border. They hadn't had word from them, and he knew there might be trouble. He knew it would be a long ride, but he also knew the enemy would attack there – the one stronghold they had been unsuccessful in finding.

Nathan knew where it was from the maps.

The pain in his side was a constant companion, but Nathan knew he couldn't let it stop him. He had to be an adult.

This filled him with pride and humility at the same time. He had come to himself. He had needed his friends, and even his enemies to better understand his purpose.

It was a few hours ride – in the dark – in the woods. Nathan had a compass and a flashlight to help in keeping on the path. Soon Nathan was fatiguing. He stopped to eat a bit and stretch his legs. He felt the sharp pain in his side reminding him of his failure. He pushed it away. He thought about his first ride with Henry and Sam. How immature he had been. How weak and fragile he had thought he was.

It was true what they said: "bad things in life make you stronger" and "it's amazing what you can get used to."

A few birds sang their early morning song. Dim light created tree monsters waving in the morning breeze. The cottonwoods sounded like a gentle waterfall. On a nice day he would have loved that sound. But today fluttering leaves masked the sounds of danger.

He wouldn't let fear creep into his heart. He focused on the aromas of the morning dew and the sound of Kane's hooves on the soft path.

Nathan emerged from the woods near the outpost. The early pink light illumined buildings, shapes of horses, shapes of men – the sentries.

Suddenly there was a shot and Nathan heard a whir past his head and a bullet hitting a tree behind him. He jumped off Kane and took cover. Kane ran for cover as well – in the opposite direction.

The jump had agitated his wound. He breathed through the pain.

Nathan crept around the north end of the outpost, counting men, counting horses. He heard voices and running. Someone had shot too soon. They were looking for him. He heard a verbal fight. The enemy had arrived ahead of him.

He heard the branches break but didn't react fast enough. Turning around with his gun ready he counted three men as they grabbed him, gagged him, and gouged him in the stomach. Then someone kicked him in the back for good measure. "We got 'em!" yelled another.

They dragged Nathan into the outpost building. Inside he saw men gagged and bound and lined up along the far wall.

"Where are the others?" snarled the first thug, pulling out the gag from Nathan's mouth.

Nathan coughed.

"That old dude, Sam, where's he at?" said the second.

"He won't talk unless you hurt him real bad," said the third.

"Let me talk to him," said another.

It was Joe.

Joe, the spy.

The other men moved aside as Joe approached Nathan.

"Nate, listen, it will go better if you just tell us who else came with you and what your plans are," said Joe, using his best friendly voice.

Nathan's mind worked on the problem of freeing the men as he pushed his anger at hearing Joe's voice off to the side.

"Did you come with Henry and Sam?" Joe paused, like a snake moving in circles, finding a way in.

"Matt!" Joe announced with authority.

"Sir."

"Did we get his horse?"

"No, Sir."

After a few expletives, Joe hissed, "Well, don't you think you should go after it?"

Two men nodded and rushed outside.

Something like hurt and disappointment tried to worm its way into Nathan's heart. Joe had become a second in command for Phil Amor, something that had never been granted to Nathan as a son. He felt sadness, loss, and pity all at once. He tried to focus on the old man and the good things he had done for the ranch and for Nathan.

He wondered what horrible things Joe had had to do to get the position he was now in.

"Gotta show you something," said Joe as he grabbed Nathan by the sleeve and pulled him outside.

Nathan searched the faces of the other prisoners as he stumbled over the threshold. They gave nothing away.

The sky was getting brighter, but no birds were singing. Joe tried to throw Nathan to the ground, but only succeeded in pushing him a few feet ahead.

"Take a look at that monster," said Joe. "You guys are through."

Growing from the shadows loomed a tank just like the ones filled with concrete sitting outside of veteran buildings all around the United States. Only this one was moving. The motor revved. Diesel exhaust filled the air. Nearby trees seemed to wilt.

Nathan felt heart sick. It seemed that his father's plan was to destroy everything. It didn't make sense, thought Nathan.

Then he remembered the words of his friend, "Since when does evil make sense?"

The top of the tank opened with a groan and Phil Amor emerged just as the sun made its appearance behind him creating the illusion of a large unidentifiable monster.

"Ethan! Great to see you! Glad you could make it to the party." Phil Amor jumped from the top of the tank like some hideous animal landing on all fours. He had a crooked smile on his face. Nathan almost didn't recognize him.

"I'm calling you by your given name, Ethan. It's the one you grew up with. It's the one that belongs on you."

Nathan set his jaw as Amor's minions gathered around him. It looked as if they had been promised entertainment.

"I have connections, Ethan, lots of connections, as you can see. That's why I need you.

"Ethan, I need you. I know it was wrong to send Bambi to kill you, I see that now. I'm sorry that you were hurt. It must be fate that you are still alive. I need you to help me make connections within the old man's ranch. We could be powerful, you and me. We could take over this whole country and live like kings!"

"I don't want to live like a king. I like my life at the ranch." Nathan's voice was muffled by the gag.

Phil Amor took three strides up toward Nathan and slid off his gag. Then he slapped him hard. "You never were a very obedient child – so rebellious. Ah, well. Too bad, I'm going to bomb the crap out of your lovely ranch."

"Why?"

Phil Amor grinned. His mouth turned down slightly on the left as if he was incapable of a complete smile, as if he had had a stroke.

Phil Amor sighed. "No one is cooperating with me. They don't share my vision. But you share my vision, don't you, Ethan. You have always shared my vision of a better place for all of us, never hungry again, lots of travel, only the best of everything."

Nathan coughed. He glanced around at the crew. Don't they see he's crazy?

"Time to wreak havoc, Jack!" announced Phil Amor. The guns of the tank turned toward the center of the ranch making a sickening squeal of metal on metal.

"Since no one will give me the coordinates for the Central Outpost I'll just bomb the Big House. I'll kill everyone inside, including the old man, and then you'll HAVE to share my vision."

With a jerk, Nathan broke free of the guard and lurched at his father, slamming him in a full body tackle. Three thugs grabbed Nathan and hit him with their fists and their guns. Nathan struggled to get free.

Suddenly shots rang out. Several thugs fell. The rest hit the dirt. Nathan followed suit and played dead as he had been trained. His hands were freed. The sun was full up, and through the dust Nathan could see bodies everywhere, some moving, some very still. In the chaos he crawled to a nearby body and pulled off a pistol.

A few more shots. Nathan checked for ammo. Full.

The tank powered down. Yelling and scuffling created a cloud of dust around Nathan. He knew he needed to lie still.

"Hey! There's Nate!" It was Henry's voice. The relief Nathan felt brought tears to his eyes. Arms lifted him and he stood on his own.

"You're alive," said Sam.

Nathan smiled. Then he saw a flash of motion in his left peripheral. He turned in time to see Phil Amor going for the gun he kept in the back of his pants. Nathan shot first. Then another shot rang out. Amor froze. Two more shots and he fell to the ground like a sack of potatoes.

Nathan rushed over to him. He turned him over. "Father," he whispered.

Phil Amor looked up at Nathan and said, "I always loved you."

"No, father, you didn't. Not really," said Nathan. "You always loved money. You always loved power. You never understood real love. I'm sorry I couldn't show you that."

"You're just a stupid kid," said Phil Amor, his voice hard. "My men will get revenge."

"No, Phil," said Nathan. "They won't. Men who fear their leader quickly switch sides."

His eyes glazed, fading. "What?"

"Never underestimate the enemy," said Nathan.

With his last breath Phil Amor cursed through clenched teeth, "Damn you."

Nathan knelt by his father until more help arrived.

Solomon worked with the other healers to help the fallen. He knelt next to Nathan.

"Nathan," he said, "I'm sorry about your father."

Nathan nodded. "I couldn't save him."

Solomon touched Nathan's side. "How is your wound?"

"Hurts a bit, Sol."

Nathan spotted Sam.

"Sam!"

"Hey, Nate," said Sam. "Were you hiding all this time?"

Nathan ignored the joke. "How did you know where to find us?"

Henry walked up from behind the tank. "This tank looks like one that had me dead to rights in the last war. Lots of noise. No accuracy. Howdy, Nate."

"Hi, Henry."

"Nate, you may be quiet, but you ain't that quiet," said Henry. Sam laughed at that.

"Oh," said Nathan. "You knew."

"Sure we knew," laughed Henry. "I could see it in your eyes. You had a plan."

"Yeah." Sam slapped Henry on the back making him wince. "'Watch Nate,' he says. 'He's cookin' up a plan,' he says."

"Good thing you guys know me so well," said Nathan.

"It made sense," said Henry. "We had lost communications with the South Post and were planning to investigate anyway. Your plan worked better than you thought."

"I really didn't have a plan," said Nathan. "I just knew something was happening and I wanted to help."

"A feeling in your bones?" asked Sam.

Nathan nodded.

"I'm sorry about your dad," said Henry.

"I don't really think he was ever my dad," said Nathan.

"You'll mourn him just the same," said Solomon.

Nathan nodded. "What's going to happen to all his men?"

They watched as Amor's men were rounded up

and placed in trucks.

"They'll be given to the sheriff and prosecuted," said Solomon. "The dead will be buried as per their families' wishes. Three are going to the hospital in the city. They don't want to be treated by us."

"What about Phil Amor?" asked Nathan.

"We don't know yet," said Solomon. "He has no family that we know of except for you. Bambi was the only one living at the mansion. Staci is with us here at the ranch. The old man will make the calls to the lawyers. Until then his body will be kept in the city morgue, along with Bambi."

Nathan struggled to think of some appropriate burial for his father. "Maybe he and Bambi should be buried on the Amor family plot on the hill behind the stables."

Solomon nodded.

"Nate, you remembered everything," said Sam.

"Just about ... and it doesn't hurt anymore."

Chapter 32

Later that week, Cook sang in the kitchen again. It was a song of strength and gratitude. The deep mourning was over.

Life on the ranch returned to normal as everyone chipped in to repair the damage the war caused.

Nathan spent a few days at the Rest House. Henry stayed a bit longer. Sam had to stay a long time since he had pushed himself so hard. It seemed like his old body was wearing out.

A few good men had died on both sides. The Old Stone Sanctuary rang bells of mourning. Music could be heard day and night. Hamilton was seen lighting candles and praying with visitors. Nathan was able to attend the memorial services.

Staci was calm and peaceful, possibly for the first time in her life. She was now living in the Rest House with Ruby and was in training to be a Listener.

Solomon lit candles for each of the men he could not save from both sides of the war. He mourned for them. He learned about them from their families if they could be found.

Henry went back to caring for the horses. He was a little slower, but the herd didn't care.

Sam tried to leave the Rest House, but the staff insisted it wasn't wise. Sam was happy there, talking to everyone he could, but he missed his Lady. Solomon assured him that he and his horse would be reunited soon.

Alex and the old man worked with the lawyers to settle the interment of bodies. Workers from the ranch were sent to Phil Amor's property to help with daily chores, caring for the animals and organizing the maintenance of his estate until the legal issues were resolved.

Chef took two days a week to fix special meals at the Phil Amor estate. Peace sometimes comes in the form of food.

Nathan picked up pen and paper and wrote a letter to Joe. He addressed it to the Phil Amor property. After he mailed the letter, he settled back in his room and read the old dusty blue book again from the beginning.

It was as if he were reading it for the very first time.

Chapter 33

Early one morning a few weeks after the last battle, Nathan sat on the porch. The old man smoked his pipe, and the sweet aroma brought a deep calm and a sweet peace to Nathan.

"Well, it's time for new duties," said the old man.

"I'm ready," said Nathan, smiling.

"Yes, you are," said the old man. "But first things first. I must tell you a story. It is one of the stories of this ranch. It is also part of your story.

"A long time ago, during the range wars and drought, I paid mortgages on several properties during that hard time. Some called me 'Land Baron,' some 'Slum Lord,' but those were the bitter ones, the ones who would not be humbled, the ones who refused to accept a simple act of kindness. They could stay if they wished, but most of them moved back east. It was tough for them, coyotes and mountain lions eating their stock, wild boar trampling their kitchen gardens, a few refusing the use a gun to protect themselves, a few refusing help from their neighbors.

"Of all those I helped, many moved on and signed their properties over to me, for which I paid full price. Some abandoned what little they had. In the end over half of those small cabins had to be torn down. Sometimes the legal fees and taxes were more than the properties were worth.

"Among those homes remaining is a small gray house not far from here. It is situated on a hill with gardens all around it. A woman lives there.

"The gray two-story has a fireplace, upstairs and down, original with the house which was built when this part of the country was still a territory. The house has been painted many colors, but today it is gray. That woman's father saved my life, Nathan. It was a brutal range war and he protected me. When she lost the rest of her family through various trials and tragedies, I let her stay there, rent free, for the rest of her life, as a thank you to what her father had done for me.

"That woman in that house has made a small fortune on herbs and medical plants. She is gifted in the gardening arts and wise in the ways of natural medicine. She has given most of what she grows to the ranch. She has taught the Healers all she knows and continues to teach what she learns. The kitchen staff uses only her trusted herbs and spices. She has earned her mortgage several times over. I have told her this, but she still refuses payment for the things she provides for us."

The old man paused to draw on his pipe. The story of the lady with the herb garden seemed familiar to Nathan somehow. In the tiniest corner of the back of his mind an aroma and the memory of a smile sparked a thought that he could not surface.

"Would you like to meet her?"

"Yes!" said Nathan.

"Well, let's saddle up."

Nathan's heart swelled with pride. At last he was riding with the old man.

It was a short thirty-minute ride. Nathan was surprised he hadn't come across the house before. It was a mere stone's throw from the southern hideout where the last battle had been fought.

"Company!" the old man called out as they approached.

Nathan got the feeling he had been here before. It was a pleasant, safe feeling, like sitting on the couch in the quiet, reading a good book.

An older lady emerged from the front door wiping her hands on her apron. She was wearing a blue gingham dress. Nathan noticed her eyes were blue too.

"Kenny!" she called. "Will you stay for coffee?"

As the two dismounted, Nathan felt like a child coming home as recognition hit him. He tried to say, "Aunt Betsie?" but the words caught in his throat. He trembled. His mouth was dry. Tears formed in his eyes. He couldn't hold them back.

The woman walked up to him and smiled.

"Elisabeth," said the old man, "this is Ethan, but we call him Nathan now. He's earned it."

"Oh, Sweety, I've missed you so," the lady whispered as she drew him into a hug.

Nathan hugged back as he erupted in sobs of relief and joy. "Aunt Betsie," Nathan whispered into her shoulder.

All this time she had been only a few miles away. Tiny snippets of memory flashed in Nathan's mind, the overnight stay grudgingly approved by his stepmother, the tears on having to go home, a day in the herb garden, his very own room, a long walk in the woods.

"Let's go inside, shall we?" said Elisabeth.

Nathan pulled away to go into the house. He wiped his eyes with his sleeve. He turned and saw his Aunt Betsie and the old man hug as if they hadn't seen each other in a long time.

"How've you been, Elisabeth?"

"Oh, good, good. I'd be better if certain people would visit more often," she chided.

"I know, I know. But, with the war ..."

"Yes, Kenny, I know. It's okay. I understand."

Nathan was staring at the woman now. Something else was happening inside his head, something primitive and deep.

"At the picnic," croaked Nathan. "At the picnic table … it was you … at my table …"

Aunt Betsie nodded and smiled. "Nathan, come into the kitchen," she said.

Nathan watched them pass him into the house, but he couldn't move.

Elisabeth walked back outside again, waiting.

"Ethan."

Now, Nathan couldn't breathe. It couldn't be. It wasn't possible.

"Ethan, come inside, Honey. Come in and sit down."

The old man was suddenly at his side helping him walk up the front steps into the house and into a chair in the kitchen.

"So, you remember," said the old man.

Nathan stared at the old man, then stared at his Aunt Betsie.

"You … you're Aunt Betsie … right?"

"Yes, Ethan. We had everyone believing I was your aunt. But you were younger then and didn't remember me. We had a go-between, so I didn't have to see him. You could only stay for a short time here, then, all of a sudden you couldn't come anymore, he took you away from me forever. I never thought I'd see you again. But Ken said I would, so I trusted him and waited."

A distant memory warmed inside his heart. A memory of hugs and kisses and songs at bedtime. Tears began to roll down Nathan's cheeks. He could barely get the word out.

"Mom … Mom … I thought you were …"

"Here, Nathan, have some coffee and a little cake," said the old man. "Don't ask any questions. Just sit for a bit. In a few minutes I'll explain what happened so you can understand."

Nathan sipped the hot coffee. He took a bite of the cake, but he couldn't taste it. His mouth was as numb as his mind. He tried not to think, letting his body catch up with his brain. He closed his eyes and tried to breathe.

"Nathan," said the old man. "You have been lied to for most of your life. You understand that."

Nathan nodded. He felt as if he was waking from a dream.

"Your mother didn't die. She ran away from a dangerous situation she could not change."

"Yes," whispered Nathan. "I see that now. She ran away to here?"

"Yes, this is where she has been all this time."

"But why didn't you tell me this before now? I don't understand how you could keep this from me."

The old man leaned back in his chair and closed his eyes. "Nathan, I'm sorry. Maybe I should have told you sooner, but somehow it never seemed the right time. I couldn't help thinking that if you knew your mother was still alive, you would have told Phil Amor. That would have been dangerous for her. You see, I let Phil Amor think she was dead. I have hidden her here."

"Oh," said Nathan. "I see." Nathan focused on the large crack in the wooden kitchen table. "I probably would have told him that time he kidnapped me. I was pretty angry that day ... and confused. I might have been tempted to yell it at him during our shootout at the southern outpost, to use it to shock him, throw him off his guard."

"Thank you for understanding, Nathan. After Phil died, I knew I could safely tell you and that Elisabeth would be safe."

"May I continue, or would you like to finish the story?" the old man said to Elisabeth.

"I think you can explain it better," said Elisabeth.

"Nathan, I believe in having no secrets, so I will tell you your true history."

"Okay," said Nathan, straightening in this chair.

"Many years ago, almost 30 years, I think, I met your mother when she came to live here at the ranch.

She helped in the kitchen."

"What?" Nathan put his hand over his mouth and looked at his mother. He began to suspect the truth.

"Yes, Ethan," said Elisabeth. "Cook taught me everything I know."

The old man paused a moment to let the words sink in.

"Nathan, you need to know that I courted her, and we fell in love. We married about a year after she arrived at the ranch."

"It was such a beautiful wedding," said Elisabeth, her eyes shining. "Everyone was so wonderful. But I didn't realize at the time that I had a rebellious heart."

"Nathan, you were born a year after we married," said Ken. "She continued to work, and everyone helped to raise you. I was so proud to have a son that I could pass my ranch to."

"Wait," said Nathan. "What about Alex?"

"Yes, Nathaniel, he is my son. His story is much older, different. He is older than you are. If you would like to know his story, you will need to ask him, okay?"

Nathan nodded.

"Then, one day, when you were only three years old, your mother ran away. I am sorry to say that I did notice there was a change in Elisabeth, but she refused to share her hurt with me."

"I was so prideful," said Elisabeth. "I knew he would help me, but I wanted to be on my own. I was young. I wanted to know if I could live a rougher life, one that wasn't safe... and that's when I met Phil."

Nathan was putting the pieces together.

"Phil Amor saw his chance," said the old man. "He knew who she was and who you were. He knew he could ruin me by taking away what I dearly loved. He took a chance, and, at the time, it paid off."

"Phil offered me a job in town," said Elisabeth. "He came to see me from time to time in the apartment he found for me even after he realized I was pregnant."

"Oh!" said Nathan. "Staci?"

"Yes, that's right. Looking back I see I exchanged one security for another, but he had me convinced I was an independent woman even as he drew me in and created a dependence on him."

"He was patient," continued the old man. "His timing has always been impeccable. He courted her cautiously, dates once a week, helping her find a babysitter for you, telling her how smart she was, how capable, how well the boy was turning out, and then, when he knew she had fallen for him, he popped the question."

"Wait," said Nathan. "Weren't you already married?"

"Yes, but I didn't tell him that and I don't think he would have cared," said Elisabeth. "And he asked me to marry him even though I was pregnant with another man's baby. I couldn't believe my good fortune."

The old man continued, "I knew, of course, but what could I do? Force her to come back? Call the sheriff? You know, Nathan, that every human is given a free will. She left because she wanted to. I knew she would return if she wanted to. To force her to come back would not make her love me or be faithful to me. She had her lessons she needed to learn."

"And boy did I learn them," said Elisabeth laughing.

"Wait, wait, wait," Nathan put his hand to his head. Then he pointed at Elisabeth. "You were the lady at that first cookout after I arrived at the ranch. You smiled at me."

"And you didn't recognize me, but I knew you hadn't started remembering your old life," said Elisabeth.

"Well, you know most of what happened after that," said the old man. "You can come visit Elisabeth any time and ask your questions. But you needed to know that Phil Amor was using you to get to me. You really did not belong to him, but you thought you did because he brainwashed you. I allowed it because I knew his true nature would be revealed. The only mistake I made was letting your mother get beaten down and almost killed."

Elisabeth smiled at the old man. "But you saved me," she said as she patted his hand.

Nathan waited through the pause. He was suddenly struck by the deep love his mother and father had for each other. They allowed each to be independent and yet remained faithful.

"As you can imagine, I had people watching your mother. One was on staff at the Amor home. They knew things were getting bad. They grabbed the chance when, after a particularly bad fight, Elisabeth packed up and left in the middle of the night, leaving you and your sister in the care of the nanny, who also worked for me.

"A Seeker was sent to find Elisabeth, and she was brought to the big house. She didn't want to live there, she was too hurt and humiliated, so I asked if she would consider living in this home until she had a chance to decide what she wanted to do."

"Ethan," said his mother, kissing him on the head. "This is a big day for me. I am so glad you came to see me. Can you ever forgive me for leaving you in the hands of that dangerous man?"

Nathan was out of his chair and hugging his mother. No words were needed.

"But didn't Phil know you were at the ranch?" Nathan said. "I mean, I thought you were my Aunt Betsie ..."

"Since he lied about Elisabeth being dead, we stuck with that story," said the old man. Phil never met Aunt Betsie. For everyone's safety you were dropped off at the old schoolhouse.

"He was not a faithful husband and, I believe, had been planning to replace your mother with another woman at some point. It was a clever lie. He allowed you to see Aunt Betsie occasionally to keep you within his influence. After a few years he prevented you from visiting because he saw her influence on you."

Nathan had a quick flash of memory of a very sad day when Phil had told him his aunt was too sick to see him anymore. Nathan also remembered it was about that time he started planning to run away from home, even though it took him years to finally go through with it.

Nathan finished his cake. Then Elisabeth invited Nathan to go upstairs to his room.

"My room?"

The old man nodded.

Nathan walked up the stairs as memories flooded back. Pictures in his mind were molding together. There was the room, the door, the bed, the window, the pleasant smell of soap and fresh breezes. And the walls were old blue. Nathan thought of when he was here, visiting his Aunt Betsie. It had been so peaceful.

He lay on the squeaky bed and looked up at the comforting crack in the ceiling. The door frame was off-center, but that was exactly as it should be. He let himself cry.

Later, as Nathan walked down the stairs, he could hear another familiar voice blending with his parents. As he appeared in the kitchen doorway, Staci said, "Ethan! I mean Nate!"

Staci and Nathan smiled as they sat at the table over a second pot of coffee. Nathan felt a memory coming on. He was standing between Phil and Staci. Phil was yelling. Staci was crying. She was only three years old. Nathan let the memory come. He wasn't sick anymore. He was just sad.

He knew there would be plenty of time to talk.

After a pleasant visit, the old man and Nathan rode back to the big house. They were leaving Staci who would spend a few weeks with her mother learning the craft of healing and growing herbs.

Chapter 34

As they left the meadow Nathan spotted a rider coming through the woods.

It was Alex.

"Go with Alex, please," said the old man, "there is something you need to see."

"Okay," said Nathan. He said his good-byes to his father and rode up to meet Alex. The brothers smiled at each other and rode together in silence.

Alex led the way into the woods in the direction of the castle. A few minutes later the back of the castle came into view.

Suddenly, Nathan was hit with a sadness. He looked at Alex. He too seemed sad. Dismounting, Nathan knew in his heart what they were going to see.

It was just as he remembered it. Inside, at the pool was Sam, standing, waiting, in full dress military WWI uniform looking younger than Nathan has ever seen him.

Nathan tried not to cry. This was a happy time for Sam. He had worked so hard for so long and now he could finally rest with no more pain.

Alex appeared next to Sam as he emerged from the pool. His buddies were waiting at the doorway of the castle banquet hall cheering and calling Sam's name. They had also been washed and given their beautiful, comfortable, white clothes.

Nathan wished he could say good-bye to Sam, but he knew the rules. Sam joined the rest laughing and shaking hands and singing and patting each other on the back as they walked into the banquet room beyond. This time Nathan could smell the rich aromas of the feast.

And that made him cry.

Nathan felt a yearning that hurt deep in his gut. He wanted to join them, to be at peace, to rest and enjoy everyone's company with no more war.

But he knew his time would come.

Chapter 35

Alex and Nathan stabled the horses and walked back to the Big House. They joined the old man and Henry who were playing chess on the porch.

Cook came out with a cup of coffee for Nathan and gave him a big hug.

"Well, ya' beat me again," said Henry. "But that's probably 'cause I'm beat. I think I'll take me a nap."

"Rest well, Henry," said the old man.

Nathan moved to Henry's seat by the old man. A slight breeze created a waterfall of leaves. Nathan felt sad and happy, calm and peaceful, all at the same time. A year ago he would not have believed this beautiful day possible.

"Nathan, you will take over for Phil Amor. The estate was left to you in his will," said the old man.

"I don't want it, I mean, I'm not ready," Nathan said.

"You showed wisdom in the heat of battle, but more importantly, you showed love."

"I shot people!"

"Did you want to shoot Bambi? No. You wanted to save her. You loved her. You had her best interests at heart while she tried to kill you. Did you want to kill Phil Amor? No. You shot him to disarm him. It was an effective move. Unfortunately, he only had murder in his heart and the men fighting at your side knew that. They had to finish the job, or you would have died.”

There was a pause as each man rolled over his own thoughts.

“How do I run an entire estate?” asked Nathan.

“You will have the best people helping you, teaching you. We will see each other often and you can ask as many questions as you like.”

“What about Alex? Shouldn't he – I mean ... He's older.”

“Alex has other jobs to do,” said the old man.

“What about Phil's men. I know some were happy to leave his employment, but most of them were sold out to him and his plan.”

“Nathan, you must remember that men who serve out of fear seldom truly respect their leader. Many were happy we came. We are using The New Building for them. They are housed there and are being trained in kindness and service. If they wish to leave, they can. They are free to go, just as you are. You should know, too, that you are free to decline this assignment. Take a day or two and think it over. Talk about it with your friends.”

Nathan nodded already planning a visit to the old gray house.

Henry came out on the porch, toothpick in his mouth, apparently choosing eating over napping. “That Cook! She's almost – I say 'almost' – a better cook than Chef!”

Henry looked at the old man. “Did he say 'yes'?”

“He's thinking it over.”

“Uhuh.”

Nathan observed the two men. The old man could trust Henry with his plans, he thought. Then it dawned on him. Henry was one of the old man's “best people.”

The old man looked far and away, over the grassy expanse. He put down his coffee cup and stood in one quick, youthful movement.

A wave of anticipation hit Nathan like a strong

wind. Someone was coming home, over the hill, a small speck bobbing up and down, up and down. The old man jumped the steps two at a time – almost flying – and ran across the vast meadow to meet him.

Nathaniel stood to watch. He put his hand on Henry's shoulder and said, "I will never get tired of seeing that."

In the kitchen Cook began to sing.

The End

Thank you to all my beta readers: Evelyn Turany, Marissa Baker, Noel Lizotte, Paul Reece, Carol Kable. I couldn't have finished this without you. You found my trying typos, my grammar guffaws, my scrambled sentences, my plot pits, and my dozy descriptions. You read this book in its primitive form and still loved it.

Thank you.

-

One thing I have asked from the Lord, that I shall seek:

That I may dwell in the house of the Lord all the days of my life,

To behold the beauty of the Lord
And to meditate in His temple.

- Psalm 27:4 NASB1995

9 781950 218998